WELCOME TO
WEIRDSVILLE

Ghost School

WELCOME TO WEIRDSVILLE

Happyland
Ghost School
Dog Eat Dog

WELCOME TO
WEIRDSVILLE

Ghost School

I. M. Strange

LITTLE, BROWN BOOKS FOR YOUNG READERS
lbkids.co.uk

LITTLE, BROWN BOOKS FOR YOUNG READERS

First published in Great Britain in 2013 by Atom
Reprinted 2013

A CIP catalogue record for this book
is available from the British Library.

ISBN 978-0-349-00126-5

Typeset in Minion by M Rules
Printed and bound in Great Britain by
Clays Ltd, St Ives plc

Papers used by LBYR are from well-managed forests
and other responsible sources.

MIX
Paper from
responsible sources
FSC® C104740

Little, Brown Books for Young Readers
An imprint of
Little, Brown Book Group
100 Victoria Embankment
London EC4Y 0DY

An Hachette UK Company
www.hachette.co.uk

www.lbkids.co.uk

With special thanks to Jan Gangsei

For Ava –

my feisty little redhead

CHAPTER 1

"Brendan! Brendan Jakes!" Mrs Priddy's stern voice broke the silence of the classroom. She had looked up from her desk and now she narrowed her eyes at me. Instinctively, I sank low in my chair. After nine years of school, and more detentions than I could possibly count, I knew nothing good could come from a teacher using my full name.

There's a reason I sit in the back row.

"Um, *me*, Mrs Priddy?" I put my hand on my heart.

1

By this point, the entire class had looked around and was gawking in my direction. Rows of smirking, expectant faces ... Well, I couldn't let my audience down. I cleared my throat.

"Not guilty, your honour!" I said, and banged my hand like a gavel on the desk.

My classmates chortled. Mrs Priddy shook her head and sighed.

"Very funny, Mr Jakes," she said. "But you need to come with me. Headmaster Malton would like to see you in his office." She clicked her computer mouse and stood up.

"Oh, right." Of course he would. I sank back down in my chair again, hoping the floor would swallow me up.

"*Now*, Mr Jakes," Mrs Priddy said.

I got up, slung my backpack over my shoulder and

trudged towards the door. A couple of my mates sniggered as I walked past. So, for good measure, I looked back, wrapped my hands around my neck and pretended to choke myself. Laughter erupted.

"Enough!" Mrs Priddy snapped. "You" – she tugged my arm – "get moving!" She led me into the hallway, shaking her head. "If I had a pound for every time I've had to escort you to the headmaster's office, I'd be a very rich woman by now!"

"But, Mrs Priddy," I pleaded, now that we were out of earshot of my classmates, "I didn't do anything! I swear!"

"Of course you didn't," she answered. "Just like you didn't cover the staff room's toilet seats with cling-film last month?"

OK, so maybe she had me on that one. But this time, I really, truly had no clue what horrible thing I was about to be accused of. Whatever went wrong in my school, I got the blame ... even the times when it wasn't my fault. "No, honestly, I—"

"Save it for the headmaster." Mrs Priddy cut me off.

I sighed and clamped my mouth shut. We rounded the corner, stepping beneath the fancy archway that led to Mr Malton's office. This part of the building was all that remained from the fire that had burned most of the school to the ground in Victorian times. Behind me, the classrooms were those modern, boxy squares built back when someone decided schools should look like prisons, or mental wards. Or both. Felt like it most of the time. But this part of the school was straight out of the olden days – all brick and wood panelling and narrow windows too high to see out of.

I wrapped my arms around myself as we walked

down the dimly lit hall. This wing was always at least ten degrees colder than the rest, which I guess suited Mr Malton just fine. He wasn't exactly the warm and fuzzy type. In fact, I'm pretty sure the guy could freeze water just by looking at it.

Mrs Priddy stopped at the headmaster's door and pushed it open. "Wait in there," she said, pointing inside. "Mr Malton will be with you in a moment."

I opened my mouth to launch one final protest, but Mrs Priddy just raised her hand, turned, and whooshed back down the hall.

It doesn't matter how many times I've been here (a lot) – the headmaster's office still gives me the creeps. I'm pretty sure no one has bothered to redecorate since the nineteenth century. Rows of dusty, old, leather-bound books line one wall. Black and white school photos hang from another. A large wooden desk sits on top of a threadbare red, green and gold rug with the school logo in the centre, while a huge, throne-like chair is perched behind the desk with an oversized portrait of the very first headmaster looming above it.

I briefly considered making a break for it, but no, I was *innocent* . . . this time, anyway.

I pinched my nose shut from the mothball smell in the room and wandered along the wall of school photos, stopping in front of the class of 1863. That was the year the school burned to the ground: every single one of the kids and teachers in the photo died in the blaze 150 years ago. In fact, 150 years ago *tomorrow* – 16 October. After spending the last two months researching the fire for my local history project, I'd become kind of an expert on the subject.

I studied the picture. The students stood in four rows, standing stiff-armed in blazers, crisp white shirts and ties. Every single one of them looked straight-faced, straight-laced and miserable. Not a smile in the bunch.

It was almost like they knew what was coming.

Except for – now that I looked closer – one kid standing in the back row. He was pulling a face, tongue lolling, eyes crossed. His tie was yanked side-ways around his neck. *Brilliant!* I'm pretty sure I would've liked that kid. Although I bet that photo-bomb got him in trouble. Like the time I pulled a moony on the school bus. Pretty hilarious, actually ... except for the two weeks of detention afterwards.

I was suddenly hit by the feeling that someone was watching me. I glanced around the empty room until my eyes settled on the huge oil painting of the school's

first headmaster, Mr Lamont. Mr Malton was bad enough, but this guy seemed like someone I wouldn't want to mess with. He looked like a younger but more psychotic version of Einstein: wild black hair shooting in every direction, beady eyes staring out from behind a set of wire-rimmed glasses, mouth pursed like he'd been sucking lemons. His arms were crossed, and he sat all king-like on a chair with pointy spires rising up from either side.

The very same chair, in fact, that was just below the painting.

I struck my best Lamont-pose – fluffed-up hair, squinting eyes, puckered lips – and began to lower myself onto the red-velvet seat of the chair, camera phone held out in front of my face.

"Brendan Jakes!" a voice boomed. "Just what do you think you're doing?"

I froze, hovering over the chair, and looked up. Mr Malton's huge bulk filled the doorframe. He strode into the room, scowling. Of course, all I could do was stare at the ridiculous comb-over of hair that went from his right ear across his shiny, bald head and down towards his left ear. It bounced when he walked: mesmerising.

"Uh, nothing, sir?" I said.

"A likely story." Mr Malton snatched my phone from my hand and tossed it into his top desk drawer, slamming the drawer shut. Mr Lamont's portrait rattled on the wall, as if in approval.

"This is just the sort of behaviour I expect from you!" Mr Malton said. "Now sit" – he narrowed his cold grey eyes at me – "*somewhere else.*"

I popped up, edged along the wall to the side of his desk and lowered myself onto the small wooden

9

chair in front of it. Mr Malton sank into the throne, leaning back, sighing and cracking his knuckles.

"Now," he said. "You're probably wondering why I've asked you here today."

Actually, not really, I thought. I'd much rather not know. But I nodded instead. Mr Malton continued.

"I've called you in for a warning," he said.

I held my breath.

"As you know, your local history project is due. *Tomorrow.*"

Phew. That was it? I let out a sigh of relief.

"I *do* know," I said. "And as a matter of fact—"

"And given the relaxed attitude you've taken with your schoolwork this year, I'd be willing to bet you haven't even started it," the headmaster continued.

"Well, actually, I have!" I exclaimed.

Mr Malton ignored me completely. "You know," he said. "I expect more from a student in Year 9."

"Actually—" I tried again.

He cut me off. Again. "Just take a look at Keira Ramone," he said. "You could learn a thing or two from her, Brendan. Let me show you something . . . " He shuffled through some papers on his desk.

I shifted around in my seat. Seriously? Keira Ramone? She'd been terrorising the school since Reception year. Until something happened to her in the summer holidays; then she started acting all twitchy, like the bogeyman was going to pop out of her locker every time she opened it. Whatever. I was nothing like her: a few harmless pranks hardly equalled stuffing people's heads down the loo, like Keira used to do.

Mr Malton held a folder in the air and waggled it around.

"This," he said, tapping it, "is Keira's report. On that abandoned amusement park. Happyplace? Happyland? The point is, she handed it in early. *Early*. And I'm very much looking forward to reading it." He slapped the folder back on the desk, glanced up at the creepy painting of Mr Lamont and sighed. "Of course, I could probably turn your attitude around in a hurry if I was allowed to dole out the punishments he could. A few swipes of the cane would do the trick . . . "

"But, Mr Malton!" I could feel the heat rising in my face, and I tucked my hands under my legs to hide my balled fists. "I *have* done my project! That's what I've been trying to tell you!"

"Really?" Mr Malton raised an eyebrow.

"Yes, really!" I said. "It's on the fire that burnt down half the school. I've been working on it for weeks!"

"Of course you have. And I'm a time traveller sent back from the future." Mr Malton rose from his stupid throne and stood over me. His comb-over flopped sideways and dangled mid-air.

"Now, you listen to me, Jakes," he said. "I expect you to turn that project in – to me – first thing tomorrow morning."

This was so unfair! Everyone else was handing it in to their form teacher! I was being singled out. Again.

He leaned in closer so I could smell his stale coffee breath. Gross. "And, if that project doesn't merit *at least* a C grade, you're going to find yourself in detention" – he lifted his finger and waggled it millimetres from my nose – "for ever!"

How come every teacher in this school had it in for me? And now I had to hand in my project to Mr Malthead himself? Well, I'd show him. My project would be something epic.

"It's time you—" Mr Malton began, but a loud chanting interrupted his rant. "Now, what is that?" He stood and cocked his head to the side.

I listened carefully. "It sounds like someone singing 'Happy Birthday', sir," I said at last.

"It's not my birthday," Mr Malton mumbled, as the singing got louder. And louder. "Grrrrr ... I've had enough of this ... Always this song ... " He ran to the door and flung it open. "Gotcha!" he said.

There was no one there.

Time to get my own back. "I can tell you who it is, Mr Malton," I said. "As long as you don't tell anyone I snitched."

14

He looked back suspiciously in my direction. "Go on, then."

I lowered my voice to a trembling whisper. "It's the Ghost of Weirville School, sir."

Mr Malton lifted his finger again and pointed down the empty hallway.

"Out!" he said. "And project! Tomorrow! On my desk! First thing!"

Mr Malton practically had smoke billowing out of his ears.

"Yes, sir." I laughed under my breath as I jumped off the chair and legged it out of the door.

I'd made it about halfway down the corridor when a strange sound stopped me in my tracks. Bells. And not the electric kind that ring here when lessons finish. More old-fashioned – like you find in churches. But there were no churches within ten miles of here.

And the old school's bell tower? Well, that had burned down. One hundred and fifty years ago.

A cold chill passed over me as the clanging echoed softly down the hallway, and goosebumps crept up the back of my neck.

As the sound of the bells died away, an old playground rhyme popped into my head

Beware the tolling of the bells

And of the danger it foretells

For those who perish by the fire

A tower to a funeral pyre.

Yeah, right! I shook my head and started walking again. I was just being stupid – too long spent reading about the fire.

I checked my watch. Last lesson was almost over and no one, certainly not Mrs Priddy, would miss me. So I ran down the hall, out of the front door and straight home. I was going to finish this project and prove to everyone – especially Mr Malton – that they were wrong about me.

Dead wrong.

CHAPTER 2

I spread the "Before" and "After" pictures of the school fire across the kitchen table. The old, faded photos had been tucked inside a black envelope in a dusty old file at the school library; it had been as if they were just waiting there for me to discover them: perfect for my project.

I needed to get them in proper order, stick them in my project folder and I was finished.

Mr Malton and his stupid threats! I had done the

project – and a pretty awesome job, too. It was weird to admit, but I had actually got into it for once. Schoolwork isn't exactly my thing, normally.

A puff of perfume wafted into the room and Mum appeared in the doorway, hair done up a mile high and sprayed immobile.

"Hi, Bren Flake." She adjusted her shawl and then practically gasped at the sight of my project on the table. "Will wonders never cease?" she said.

"I work hard on all sorts of stuff."

"Oh, I know you do," she said, but she didn't look sure. She changed the subject by raising a sparkly handbag at me. "OK, then. Dad and I are going to have dinner after the play. Won't be back till late."

"Yes, Mum," I said, turning back to my project.

"You're in charge," she said. "Keep an eye on your

sister. And that doesn't mean just let her watch television all night!"

"OK." I nodded.

"And don't forget her pea—"

"I know, Mum," I said. "'Don't forget her peanut
allergy.'"

Mum was always on about Freya's peanut allergy. I
wasn't an idiot. And it was years since I had spread
peanut butter all over Freya's favourite doll. I would
never do *that* again.

"OK then, be good." Mum blew a couple of kisses in
my direction and left.

Seconds later, my eleven-year-old nightmare of a sister
bounded into the kitchen, red curls springing wildly
around her face. She clutched a thick poetry book and a
stack of teeny-bopper magazines, all cut to shreds. She
dumped them on the table. My photos flew into the air.

"Hey, watch it, Fraidy-cat!" I said, scrambling to pick up the pictures.

Freya glanced over. "Whatcha doing?"

"My project," I answered.

"You and your stupid project," she said with a giggle. "Every day at the library. Who died ... who started the fire ... it's all you ever think about. You're obsessed!"

I watched her pick up a magazine and begin snipping out a picture of her latest boy-band obsession. "Oh, yeah, like you're one to talk," I said. "Watch out, or you might chop off Harry's head. Don't you have homework or something?"

"Did it already," she said.

"Then go to bed, would you?"

Freya rolled her eyes and began clipping again. "It's only seven o'clock. And since when do you care

whether I go to bed, anyway? I swear, this project has turned you into a right swot."

"Has not."

I carefully spread my pictures out in a line again. Maybe I'd put the one of the school before it burned first, then this one that showed the fire damage, then the photo of Mr Lamont. No, wait, maybe I'd do it the other way. I rubbed my head and started again. I had to get this just right; for some weird reason, it felt like my whole life depended on this project. Well, after that meeting with Mr Malton this morning, I supposed it sort of did.

A small caption at the bottom of the Lamont photo read, "Prize Day, 1863". He stood in front of the school's iron front gates, arms crossed firmly over his chest. From everything I'd read, the guy was a complete tyrant and a total science freak, but he also believed a healthy mind required a healthy body. Looking at the thick muscles on his arms, I wasn't surprised to have learnt he pushed PE as much as he had done. I was pretty sure, too – judging by the stern look on his face – that I wouldn't have wanted to be around back then to see just how hard he pushed. No wonder all the kids in the school photo looked so miserable.

I placed Mr Lamont's photo at the front of my line-up. Perfect! All I had to do now was get Freya out of my hair, glue in my pictures and I'd still have time for a game on the Xbox.

I grabbed my backpack and reached inside.

Huh?

My project folder wasn't there.

That was odd. I looked in every pocket.

Still not there.

How was that possible? I knew I had put it in there

before my last lesson. There was no way I left the thing in my locker, was there? What if it fell out on the way home from school? I frantically shook my bag upside down. Something shuffled inside. I shook harder.

A black envelope fluttered silently to the table, landing upside-down in front of me. It was just like the one in which I'd found the old pictures. But this one was still sealed shut. Weird.

The sound of Freya whistling made me jump.

"Freya!" I said. "Shut up!"

Freya tutted. "You know what your problem is? You just don't appreciate good music."

"You know what your problem is?" I said. "You're tone deaf."

With a shaking hand, I reached out and flipped the envelope over. "Brendan" was written across the front in blood red. Every hair on the back of my neck stood

on end. No idea why. It was just an envelope, wasn't it?

I glanced over my shoulder at Freya, who was still whistling and snipping, then back at the envelope in my hands. As I tore it open, a black card slipped out. I lifted it up in front of my face. The note was hand-written, really neatly.

You left your project at school.

Oh, ha ha. I exhaled and chucked the black card across the table. One of my dumb friends playing a trick on me: Freya wasn't the only one giving me grief about geeking out on this whole project thing.

"I don't believe this!" I said, giving my bag one more useless shake. "Malt-head's going to kill me!"

Freya looked up from her cutting-out project; some Muppet-faced boy singer dangled from the edge of her scissors. I had no clue how she could spend so

much time cataloguing every move of some stupid band and still get straight As. Totally annoying.

"Oh, yeah?" she said. "What did you do now? Launch a stink bomb in your art lesson?"

"No," I said. "It's my project. It's not in my backpack. And if I don't hand it in to Mr Malton first thing in the morning I'm going to land in detention. *For ever.*" I chucked my bag on the floor and dropped my face in my palms.

"Oooooh, an eternity in detention," Freya said. "Have fun. I'll miss you."

"Shut up," I said.

"OK, OK," she said. "As nice as it would be to have the TV all to myself, how about I help you?"

I peeked through my fingers. "Help me? How?"

"Easy. I'll just whip off a new project for you. Only take me a few hours. Probably come out better

than yours, anyway. Wouldn't be hard." She put down her scissors and grinned. "All you have to do in return is take me and my mates to the Side Street concert next month. Wearing an 'I love Harry' T-shirt."

"Dream on," I said. I wasn't about to spend an entire night with a bunch of screaming eleven-year-old girls, let alone have Freya do my work for me. Besides, I was actually proud of this project. I *had* put in hours on it.

Just my luck the one time I work hard on something it gets messed up. Not even my fault, either.

I could always tape the pictures in first thing in the morning when I got to school, I realised, but that wasn't what worried me. Someone had taken my project. What if it wasn't in my locker at all? What if I couldn't find it? I'd have to start all over again.

There was only one thing to do: I had to go back to school and find my project.

"C'mon, Frey," I said.

"C'mon where? I told you I'm not tired."

"Not to bed." I stood. "To school." I told myself that it was the responsible thing to do, to bring my sister with me. I was supposed to be babysitting her, after all. It had nothing to do with wanting some company. Absolutely nothing.

"Are you crazy?" Freya said. "Mum and Dad would go ballistic!"

"It's not going to kill you to break a rule just once in your life. Come on." I scooped up my pictures and tucked them in my sweatshirt pocket. Then I headed upstairs, Freya trailing at my heels.

"What if Mum and Dad find out?" she said. "We'll be grounded for ever!"

28

"Better than lifetime in detention with Malt-head," I said.

"Yeah, for *you*," Freya said.

I dodged into my room and stuffed a bunch of pillows under my covers, arranging them until they formed the perfect Brendan-shaped lump. I leaned back to check how it looked and crossed my arms over my chest satisfied.

"Now go do the same thing to yours!" I instructed Freya.

Freya just stood there and tapped her foot. "Right," she said. "Of course I will. Now about the concert ..." That annoying smirk crept across her face again.

"Yeah ... OK. Whatever." I'd find a way to dodge that bullet later.

She scuttled off to her room and met me back in

the hallway, wearing a Side Street hoodie and carrying a bag of pick'n'mix.

"Not any peanuts in that, are there?" I said. "Mum said I have to keep you safe."

Freya groaned. "Do I look completely stupid?"

We slipped outside into the dark night. The street was dead quiet. Wind whistled up the path. The door blew shut behind me.

There was no danger from peanuts. But it still felt anything but safe.

CHAPTER 3

"And then," said Freya, as we walked back towards school, "there are the bells that clang every Wednesday just before two. Even though the bell tower burned down, like, a gazillion years ago."

"Uh-huh," I said, trying to ignore her ramblings – and the fact I had heard bells ringing today. Just before two. It had to be a coincidence. Or someone messing around. Or . . . whatever.

A cold mist had settled over town, giving everything

a hazy, dream-like look. It didn't matter what time of year it was, the clouds always clung to Weirville like a soggy tissue. One of the many reasons people call this place Weirdsville, I guess.

Freya and I made our way down the street, past dimly lit houses with television screens flickering inside. Man, this was so uncool: I was the one who should be chilling in front of the TV! When I worked out who'd played this trick on me, they were going to be sorry they picked Brendan Jakes to mess with.

"And," Freya continued, getting all dramatic now, "how about the wind that blows through the science lab, even on perfectly still days ... the gym equipment that falls to bits for no reason ... the footsteps running down the hall ... the smell of smoke ... " She threw another handful of sweets into her mouth.

"Yeah, yeah," I said. "Got to be the Ghost of Weirville School."

The school came into view, rising from the gloom on the hill straight ahead. I could just make out the metal spires of the main gate and the top of the old part of the school poking above the haze.

"And don't forget the manic sounds of 'Happy Birthday' being sung in the library!" Freya said.

I grinned to myself when I thought of Malt-head shouting "Gotcha!" to an empty corridor. Then another thought hit me. Of *course*! Whoever was playing that trick on Mr Malton – singing outside his room – must've been the one who took my project. They'd have heard his ultimatum. My fists clenched. I'm all for practical jokes, but this was a step too far.

We walked along the tangled path alongside the

33

school's wrought-iron fence. Straight ahead, I could see the place where the old bell tower once stood; a circle of charred bricks was all that remained to mark the spot. And as it was after midnight now – it was 150 years ago *today*.

Freya began to hum "Happy Birthday".

"Seriously, Frey. Shut it!" I said.

She giggled. "Who's the fraidy-cat now?"

We reached the main entrance and stopped. The tall black gate towered above us, the letters "WS" engraved in the old metal. A heavy chain and padlock hung from the railings. I yanked at them anyway. The lock and chain only rattled in response.

"Oh, well," Freya said. "Guess it's lifetime in detention for you!"

"Let's try the side gate," I said.

We squeezed our way down the narrow trail. Trees grew alongside, the branches getting closer and closer to us the further we went. It began to feel like one was going to reach down and grab me. I shook that thought from my head. I was letting Freya get to me. Where was that gate, anyway?

Finally, I spotted it straight ahead, half hidden by some shrubbery. I approached, arm outstretched. Before I could even touch the handle, the thing swung open with a creak. I jumped back a step, heart thumping and looked around. Odd. No one here. No wind even . . .

"Ooooh," Freya said. "It's the Ghost of Weirville School."

"Yeah, right," I said. I spun around, arms raised. "Boo!"

Freya yelped and dropped her pick'n'mix.

"Not funny!" she said, picking up her bag, half her sweets scattered on the ground.

"Serves you right," I said. "Now let's get this over with."

Dead leaves crunched beneath our feet as we walked through the empty courtyard, and wind whistled through the trees. Although the interior of the school was pretty up to date, the exterior of the huge brick building had been rebuilt to look just like the old school: a tall, rectangular entryway rose from the centre, on either side of which long wings with arched windows extended into the darkness. A series of triangular peaks formed the roofline like rows of jagged teeth.

As we got closer, I noticed a light shining from one of the downstairs classrooms. I stopped and grabbed Freya by the arm.

"Oh, no!" I pointed. "Someone's still here."

Freya shrugged. "Maybe someone just forgot to turn off the light."

We crept carefully along the building towards the illuminated window and stopped. I put my finger to my lips, stood on my tiptoes and peeked inside, expecting to see the caretaker or one of the teachers staying late to do some marking.

"There's no one in there," I whispered to Freya.

"See?" she said.

I stepped on a large stone in the flowerbed beneath the window and pulled myself up higher. My forehead had barely brushed the glass of the window when the latch slipped from the lock and clattered onto the windowsill. The window yawned open with a groan and a cold breeze hit me in the face.

"Whoa!" I said, jumping down and catching my breath.

"What did you just do?" Freya said.

"Guess I must've bumped it." I glanced up at the open window, trying to work out how I had knocked it loose.

"Brendan," a voice whispered.

"What is it now?" I spun around and looked at my sister.

"What?" said Freya. "I didn't say anything."

"Ha ha." I shook my head. "Follow me." I reached up, grabbed the windowsill with both hands and swung my leg over with a grunt. My sweatshirt snagged on the latch. I wriggled myself loose and dropped into the room, then glanced back at my sister.

She stood there silently, chewing her bottom lip.

"Not starting to believe your own stories now, are you, *Fraidy-cat*?" I reached my hand down to her.

Freya stuck her tongue out, grabbed hold of me and hoisted herself through window.

We were in one of the Reception classrooms. Brightly coloured letters and numbers decorated the walls above a row of computers. Picture books were arranged in baskets next to a circle of small chairs. A hamster ran around like mad in his cage, sending sawdust flying in every direction. It squeaked as we passed by.

"Sorry, mate!" I said.

I opened the door and peeked down the hallway. Empty.

"All clear!" I said. Freya and I walked quickly through the darkened corridor. The Year 9 lockers

lined the wall at the very end. I stopped at mine. Heart pounding, I twirled the combination, with each click praying my project was still inside. The lock popped open and I yanked at the door.

My folder tumbled out and landed at my feet.

I picked it up and flipped through the pages. OK, there was the early history of the school, the old map, the fire and the rebuilding. I felt my heart rate calm down. Everything was there. *Phew!* Now I could go home, add my pictures and be done. And when I found out who'd played this prank on me, there'd be trouble. Keira Ramone, maybe. This was just the sort of trick she'd pull.

"Can we get out of here now?" said Freya. "Before Mum and Dad get home!"

I nodded. But, as I turned to leave, my foot snagged on a loose tile poking up from the floor. I fell and

landed on my knees, my project skidding across the hallway.

While Freya scrambled to retrieve my folder, I looked down at the floor. The tile had come completely loose. Great. Now I could add "Destroying school property" to my growing list of offences. I was about to jam the tile back into place when I noticed something sticking out from the hole it had left.

"Huh?" I reached down and wriggled loose a crumpled black envelope. Another one? Really? With a gulp, I ripped it open. A large, old-fashioned key fell to the floor with a *clink*, and a scrap of yellowed paper fluttered down after it.

"Awww," Freya said. "Isn't that sweet? The ghost left you a present!"

"Don't be stupid," I said. "It's obviously just part of

the joke." I picked up the paper and found a message written in that same, super-neat handwriting:

You might find this useful - D.

"What is it?" Freya said.

"Not a clue." I shrugged and dropped the key and note in my pocket. "D"? Not Keira Ramone then.

We were halfway to the classroom when I remembered something.

"Wait!" I said. "My phone! It's in Malt-head's office. Let's get it."

Freya groaned. "You are seriously going to owe me," she said. "If Mum catches us, I'm not going down for you!"

"Yeah, yeah," I replied. "But imagine what Malt-head will do when he realises my phone's gone. He'll think he's lost it and then he'll have to buy me a new one!"

"I'm beginning to think *you're* the one who's lost it," Freya said.

We walked down the silent hall, past the rows of lockers and darkened classrooms, towards Mr Malton's office. Freya slowed when we reached the old archway. Wood-carved flowers and vines crept along the sides, capped by a set of twin cherubs on top. Well, they were cherubs judging by their feet and bodies, at least – their once-angelic faces had been singed away by the fire, leaving behind just two vacant ovals to watch over the students.

I grabbed Freya's arm and pulled her through to the other side. Another blast of cold air washed over me. This place had a serious draught problem. I wrapped my arms around myself, got to Mr Malton's door and pushed it open with my foot.

The office was dark, illuminated by just a sliver of

43

moonlight slanting in sideways from the high window. It fell straight across the school picture from 1863, lighting the faces of all the children. The dead ones. I looked away.

"Hurry up," Freya said, face pale. I was about to tease her, but she looked too freaked out. Instead, I strode across the room to Mr Malton's oh-so-precious chair, hovered over it . . .

. . . and let one rip.

Freya laughed. Now that was more like it!

I reached for Mr Malton's desk drawer but, suddenly, out of nowhere, the room seemed to shift beneath my feet. I felt like I was spinning. I lost my balance and fell backwards into the chair.

"Whoa, Frey, did you feel—?"

CLANG! CLANG! CLANG!

My words were interrupted by the deafening

sound of a bell. A real bell: not just some distant echo. It couldn't be – could it? I stood shakily. Freya was at the door, eyes screwed shut, hands over her ears.

I ran and grabbed her by the elbow.

"Forget the phone!" I said. "Let's go!"

We rushed back down the hallway and back into the new part of the school. But this time, the cold air clung to my skin.

I couldn't wait to get out of this place, and hurried on. But where was Freya?

Looking back, I could see that, for some reason, she had come to a dead stop at the doorway to her classroom.

"Come on!" I shouted.

She just shook her head.

"I thought you wanted to get out of here!"

She shook her head again.

I retraced my steps to see what she was staring at. "What the ...?"

Freya looked at me, eyes wide.

I stared into the Year 7 classroom in disbelief. All of the metal desks were gone, replaced by antique wooden ones with ink wells on top. The white boards were now blackboards. There wasn't a computer in sight. And, now that I noticed it, the hallway was empty of lockers, too. I swallowed the dry lump forming in my throat.

I recognised this place.

And it wasn't my school.

Well, it *was* my school – but it was the one that had stood here 150 years ago. Before burning to the ground.

Pulse quickening, I turned and looked back at the

archway. The angels stared back at me mockingly from their un-singed eyes, creepy smiles plastered serenely across their perfectly smooth faces.

What was going on?

CHAPTER 4

"I don't like this," Freya said.

"Me, neither."

A cold gust blew up the hallway again, followed this time by the sound of feet scraping across the floor. I turned slowly.

A neat line of school children rounded the corner, single file, shuffling down the hall dressed in crisp, clean uniforms. Their eyes stared straight ahead; they didn't smile – just like the kids in the old school photos from Mr Malton's office. In fact, as they got closer, I could see they were *exactly* like the kids in the photos – black and white, without a hint of colour: it was like watching an old newsreel flicker past. I wondered if I could put my hand right through one of them, but I was afraid to try.

"Hey, mate," I said to the nearest one. "What are you doing here?"

He didn't say a word. In fact, none of the drone-like children even turned to look at me. They just kept marching.

"Who are you?" I said.

No answer.

"Hello!" I yelled, right at the side of another kid's monochrome face. "Where are you going?"

He didn't so much as blink.

I took a step back. "What is going on here?" I said to

my sister. "Why can't they see us? Are they ... " I gulped. "Ghosts?"

Freya tugged my sleeve. "I don't know. But do you really want to stick around and find out?"

"Good point," I said.

We ran in the opposite direction, heading straight toward the main exit. I knew it would normally be alarmed at this time of night, but setting one off was about the last thing on my mind at this point. Until a voice cut through the sound of our running feet.

It sounded like a boy, barking out orders. My muscles tensed – if those kids were ghosts, how could one of them be talking?

"Straighten your ties!" the boy yelled. "Stand tall! Don't look at me, look ahead! Now, march in time ... " He stopped abruptly. "What is that sound?" he said. "Is someone running in the hallway?"

Freya and I slowed and looked at each other.

"Does he mean us?" she said.

I shrugged. We ran faster.

I could feel someone – or something – right behind me.

"You!" An ice-cold hand reached out and grabbed my ear. I spun around, finding myself face to face with one of the black and white kids. His slick hair looked like it had been parted down the middle with a ruler and he wore a crisp school uniform, just like the others. Except this boy's monochrome blazer had a shiny prefect badge pinned to the front.

The prefect sized me up, sneering down his long nose. "There is *no* running in the halls!" he snapped. "And where are your uniforms? These are not school approved!" He flicked my sweatshirt. "You look like vagabonds!"

My mouth opened, but for the first time in my life I couldn't come up with anything clever.

"You are lucky Mr Lamont didn't catch you," the prefect continued. "It would have been a caning for both of you!"

"Lamont? Who is Mr Lamont?" Freya said.

"The headmaster," I said with a gulp. "From one hundred and fifty years ago." I shuddered, picturing the crazed portrait of Mr Lamont staring down at me in Malt-head's office this morning. "You know, mad scientist. On steroids."

"This can't be real, right?" Freya said. "This kid can't exist. None of them can!"

The prefect shot Freya an irritated look, and then grabbed us both by the collar. For someone who didn't exist, he was freakishly strong.

"You two troublemakers are coming with me!" He

dragged us down the hall. We went past classrooms filled with more of the monochrome students. They sat behind small desks, staring dead ahead, scraping chalk across their slates in unison. Not one turned or looked up.

This had to be a dream. A really bad one.

"Ow!" I said, as the prefect yanked me sideways towards a cupboard marked "Lost Property".

"Here we are," he said. He let Freya and me go with a little shove and flung open the cupboard door. Piles of old blazers, ties and book bags were spilled on the floor. The prefect began rooting through them.

"Ooooh, not Slytherin, not Slytherin ... " I said, rubbing my neck.

Freya guffawed.

The prefect glanced up at me and scowled. "Pardon me?"

"Nothing," I said.

The boy shoved a pair of grey blazers and ties in our faces. "Put these on," he said.

"I can't believe we're actually taking orders from someone who isn't even here," Freya muttered, as she shoved her bag of pick'n'mix into a pocket of her blazer.

"Uniforms! Now!" the boy barked.

I folded my project into the inside pocket of my own blazer and slipped it over my shoulders.

Instantly, my body seemed to freeze. I looked at Freya. I could have sworn her skin was growing paler, her red hair dimming, her blue eyes fading to grey. She closed them tight.

"This is not real, this is not real," she said.

The prefect's lips drew together in a tight line. "Not real?" he snapped. "Not real? I'll show you what's real."

He marched us to the main doors and kicked them

open. The bitter air outside made my eyes water. We stepped into the mist, which still hung low over the grounds, only now it had grown even denser, making it impossible to tell whether it was day or night.

I strained to see two metres ahead. The wind howled and rattled against the distant fence.

"Where's he taking us?" Freya whispered.

"I don't know," I said. "Hopefully out of this place."

No such luck.

We came to a stop in front of a circular brick building I had never seen before. I peered up into the fog. The building narrowed as it got taller; a metal dome sat on top. What was this thing?

I glanced back towards the school, then at the fence, then to where we stood. Suddenly, it hit me. The centre of the courtyard. The circle of bricks. With a shiver, I realised what we were standing beneath.

The bell tower.

Still intact.

The prefect pulled at a small black door. It opened with a creak. He pushed us inside and pointed at a spiral staircase that wound straight up into darkness. I hesitated.

"Move, you wretch!" the prefect said.

I took a step onto the stairs and the wood groaned beneath my feet. Freya followed close behind.

"Hurry along now. Chop chop!" the prefect ordered. I looked over my shoulder to see him poking my sister in the back. She was chewing her lower lip again, her arms folded tight across her chest, and she was trembling.

My hands balled into fists. This was getting out of hand. Nobody pushed my little sister around. Except me. "Hey!" I started to say, but the sudden sound of bells drowned out my voice. I slapped my hands over my ears. It was the same bell I'd heard this afternoon and in Malton's office earlier. Only this bell was louder. And creepier. Like a death knell shaking my bones.

The clanging stopped, only to be replaced by the sound of a child wailing. My breathing got faster. I inhaled deeply a few times and tried to rub away the goosebumps creeping up my arms. Freya grabbed the back of my blazer.

"I want to go home!" she hissed. "Now!"

"Home?" the prefect laughed. "Not until you've served your punishment." He shoved Freya and she bumped into me. I nearly fell.

Reluctantly, we stumbled our way up the circling staircase and, finally, took the last few steps to the top. The prefect snaked his arm around us and lifted the latch to another black door. It groaned open and I squinted into the darkness, just making out the shape of a huge bell dangling in the centre of a circular room. Instinctively, I took a step back.

"Get inside!" The prefect shoved us forwards. Something rustled in the rafters and flew across the ceiling. Freya let out a small cry.

I'd had enough. I spun around, nose to icy nose with the prefect, who stood in the doorway with his hands on his hips.

"OK, get out of my way," I said.

"Where, precisely, do you think you're going?" he said.

"Out of here!" I gave him a shove. His body was like a brick wall.

"You are not going anywhere until you have completed your punishment."

"Who made you the boss?" said Freya.

The prefect glared at her, tapped the badge on his chest and pointed at a stack of papers and pencils tossed in the corner. "You must write out the lines: 'I will not run in the corridor, nor disregard the school uniform, nor disobey the school rules.' A million times."

I couldn't help the laugh that escaped my lips. "Nice one. That's insane."

The prefect smiled. "Headmaster's rules."

"You can't be serious," said Freya. "That'll take, like, years!"

"Better get started then," he said. He walked back out of the door, slamming it shut.

I heard a key scrape in the lock, then footsteps disappearing down the stairs. The room went deathly silent, as if all the air had been sucked out.

I threw myself at the door and yanked on the handle till my arms ached and my heart was pounding in my ears.

Freya tried too, then sank back, defeated. "We're not getting out of here," she said.

I looked at the looming shape of the bell, eerily silent, then at the papers and pencils.

"Better start—"

A muffled sob interrupted me. I held my breath and listened.

A nervous whimper trickled from the shadows.

I glanced at Freya. Apparently we weren't alone.

CHAPTER 5

Freya gripped my arm. "What is that?" she whispered. "Another ghost?"

I really wasn't sure any more.

Freya clung to my sleeve as we crept slowly around the bell. Dust puffed up from the creaky floor with every step and I held back a sneeze. We stumbled our way around to the other side of the dome. As we did so, the sobs grew louder. Freya's nails dug into my arm.

"Ouch, Frey!" I shook her loose.

"Sorry."

I stopped and pushed a huge cobweb away. A boy sat facing the far wall, head down, hands over his eyes, wearing a pointed hat. Sheets of paper were scattered all about. His shoulders shook as he wept.

I cleared my throat. "Hello," I said, trying to keep my voice from cracking. "Are you OK over there?"

The boy turned, dropping his hands from his face and pushing himself to his feet. He was ghostly pale and in uniform, like all the strange kids marching through the halls. Dark circles ringed his eyes. The tall hat on his head had a huge "D" on the front.

The boy sniffled and wiped his face. "Pardon me," he said, clearing his throat. "A speck in my eye. The dust."

"Yeah, right, definitely," I said. I'd be embarrassed, too, if someone had caught me bawling in a corner.

I looked at the boy's face as Freya and I made our way towards him. He was probably twelve or so and looked vaguely familiar. I just couldn't work out why.

"Who are you?" I said.

"Daniel Mason."

"Oh," I said. "Is that what the 'D' on your hat is for?"

The boy raised an eyebrow. Freya leaned over and whispered. "It's for 'Dunce', you dunce!"

"Oh, right. I knew that," I said. "So, what are you doing here, Daniel? Was that you ringing the bell?"

The boy shook his head. "I've got detention."

"Classic," I said. "What are you in for?" I was still trying to place him.

"Pulled a face. During the school photograph," he said. His shoulders slumped, but a satisfied grin spread across his face for an instant.

"That's it!" I said. "That's how I know you! I recognise you from that photo in Mr Malton's office!" I gave him a hearty thump on the back. "Nice work!"

Daniel looked confused. "You've seen the photo? But it was only taken today. And who's Mr Malton?"

A sudden crack of thunder rumbled across the sky, shaking the bell tower. Lightning briefly illuminated the dark shadows, outlining the spider webs, bat nests and other nasty things that had set up home here. A horrible thought crossed my mind.

"Wait a minute," I said. "What day is it today?"

"The sixteenth of October," Daniel said.

"No, I mean what year?" I asked shakily.

"Have you lost your marbles?" He blinked a few times. "It's 1863."

Freya and I looked at each other. It was 16 October

1863. The exact day that fire had burned our school to the ground! And, here we were, locked in the bell tower – which had been reduced to rubble.

The night was going from bad to worse.

"How did it start?" Freya whispered to me. "The fire?"

In all my research, that was the one thing I had not found out – what had actually caused the school to go up in smoke.

There was another bang in the sky overhead and the floor shook. Another quick burst of light reflected across my sister's pale face. Her eyes flashed fear and she squeezed my arm again.

"I don't know," I said. "But maybe it was lightning. Which means we need to get the heck out of here before we're burned alive!"

"Burned alive?" Daniel said. "What in the devil are

you talking about? Who are you, anyway? Are you new?"

"I'm Brendan," I said. "This is my sister, Freya." I nodded to the door. "Don't suppose you have the key, do you?"

"Of course," Daniel said. "I've *chosen* to remain shut in this place."

I was about to congratulate him on his sarcasm when I remembered something. "Wait!" I said. "He may not ... but maybe I do!" Freya raised her eyebrow. I pulled the mystery key from my pocket: the one that had come in the black envelope. "Let's give this a try!"

"Yes!" Freya said.

Daniel looked curiously at the old key in my hand. "Where did you find that?"

"Under a loose tile in the hallway. Had a note attached. Said it might come in handy." Quickly, I hustled us all back around the bell to the door. I pushed the key into the lock.

It slid all the way in. *Yes!*

I gave it a slow turn.

One click. Two clicks ...

I waited for the lock to catch.

But the key just kept turning in the hole. *Useless.*

"Great." I stuffed it back in my pocket. "So now how are we supposed to get out of here?"

"That's simple," Daniel said.

"It is?" I asked hopefully.

"Certainly. All we have to do is write our lines. A million times." His shoulders slumped again.

Well, that wasn't the answer I had been looking for. Now we were going to be stuck here for ever. Or until we went up in flames. Neither option sounded too appealing.

"Hold on!" Freya said. "I have an idea!"

She ran across the room, grabbed a sheet of paper and pressed it against the wall. I watched her write, "*I will not run in the corridor, nor disregard the school uniform, nor disobey the school rules.*"

"OK, Frey, I know you're a fast writer, but that's going to take for ever!"

Freya just grinned and tacked the words "*A million times*" to the end of her line.

The lock clicked, the latch creaked and the door swung open.

"Unbelievable," I said. "How can that possibly have worked?"

She dropped the paper and ran into the stairwell. Daniel and I tried to follow but, before we could make it out of the door, a huge gust of icy wind blew us back inside and the door slammed closed.

I landed in a pile of dustballs. *Yuck.* I stood and shook the dirt from my clothes as wind howled through the room. The bell groaned on its axle. The scattered paper lifted into the air and twirled in circles.

"What now?" said Daniel, picking himself up from the floor next to me.

"Maybe we have to write our lines, too," I said. Another clap of thunder. Only, this time, the lightning was directly overhead and something cracked and fell on the roof above. "Hurry!"

Daniel and I scrambled to the papers, each grabbing a sheet.

I quickly scrawled the line as the wind howled. As soon as I had finished, it died down and the door opened.

Daniel glanced at me, grinning.

"Here goes nothing!" I ran through the doorway and Daniel followed.

Freya was waiting for us on the stairs. "About time!"

We bounded down the steps two at a time and bolted out of the tower. Outside, the mist was still thick, despite the fact that the wind had picked up again. The thunder boomed and lightning briefly outlined the massive school building against the bright sky – a dark shadow of turrets, spires and peaked rooflines. Then everything went dark again.

From somewhere inside, I thought I could hear voices chanting out multiplication tables: "*One times two is two; two times two is four; three times two is six . . .* "

"OK, I've officially had enough of this weirdness!" I said. "Let's go home!"

70

Freya nodded and we ran straight towards the main gate.

Daniel jogged alongside us. "Wait!" he said. "You spoke of a fire! We should warn the other children."

"How?" Freya said. "They can't hear us. They're ghos—" She stopped and studied Daniel's pale face.

"What?" he said.

"Never mind," I said. "There's nothing we can do – it's history. And we need to get out of here before we're history, too!"

CHAPTER 6

We ran to the main gate. I glanced up at the lines of wrought iron; somehow, it seemed to have grown even taller since we arrived earlier. I rattled the padlocked chain again.

"Still locked," I said.

"Yeah, no kidding," Freya said. "How about the key?"

"Right! Duh!" I reached for the key and jammed it in the lock.

This time, it wouldn't even turn.

I yanked the key out and dropped it back in my pocket, wondering why I even bothered to hang on to the useless thing. I kicked the gate in frustration, and the lock rattled mockingly.

"Let's try the side gate," I said.

We hurried along the fence, shuffling through the undergrowth and dead leaves until we reached the smaller gate. I peered through to the other side and my heart sank: I couldn't see a thing through the mist. It was almost like the entire town of Weirville and everything I knew had simply disappeared – swallowed whole by the heavy fog.

All that was left standing was this old school. And if Daniel was right about the date, even the school wouldn't be standing for long.

I reached out, hoping the gate would magically

swing open like it did when we got here. Instead, the latch creaked down and clicked into place.

"Did you see that?" I said.

Freya and Daniel both nodded. I reached out a shaking hand and squeezed the handle as hard as I could.

"It's stuck," I said.

"But there's not even a lock!" Freya said.

"Perhaps we should return to lessons," Daniel said, "before we are caught and caned."

"What?" I said. "Are you crazy? No way. Didn't you hear what I said before? This place is going up in smoke! We're getting out of here."

I wiped the sweat from my brow and studied the fence. A tangle of ivy crept from the base all the way to the top, forming the perfect foothold. I jammed my foot in the twisting stems, reached as high as I could and hoisted myself up.

74

"What are you doing?" Freya said.

"Going over!"

But when I tried to take another step, my foot wouldn't budge.

"What the . . . ?" I said. I looked down at my right foot. It was covered in leaves and vines. I could barely see my shoe. I wiggled my leg. Suddenly, the vines sprang to life, twisting and turning like snakes; the entire fence seemed to be writhing around me. Tough stems grabbed my ankles. I struggled to break free, but with every move I became more entwined, as though I was stuck in one of those trick Chinese finger traps that tighten the more you pull free.

"Get! Off! Me!" I yelled as the vines pulled me tight to the fence.

"Brendan!" Freya shrieked. "Look out!"

I glanced back at my sister and followed the path of her wide-eyed stare. A massive stem covered in thorns and leaves was creeping towards me.

"No!" I yelled, thrashing. But it was no use. The vine curled itself around my waist, squeezing the breath right out of me. It wound its way up my chest, with every passing second inching closer and closer to my neck. It was trying to kill me!

I began to feel lightheaded and tiny spots of light obscured my vision. I was vaguely aware of Freya and Daniel yelling, grunting and pulling at the vines, my legs and feet.

"Let go of my brother!" Freya said.

"It's too strong!" Daniel said. "We need something else!"

I was distantly aware of a scraping sound behind me, but then my ears began to ring, replaced by the sound of a rhythmic thumping: the blood coursing through my ears.

For the very last time.

A set of hands landed on my back. Just as I was about to lose consciousness, an arm slipped around my waist and yanked me down. I fell with a thud.

Freya and Daniel stood over me, wide-eyed. Daniel held a jagged stone in his right hand. The large vine lay on the ground, severed in half.

"Brendan!" Freya threw her arms around me. "I thought you were going to die!"

I gasped for breath. "Me, too." I nodded at Daniel. "Thanks, mate."

"Um ... my pleasure." He dropped the stone and wiped his palms on his trousers.

Freya let go of me. "Well, now what?" she asked shakily.

"I think it's safe to say this place doesn't want us to leave," I said.

"But if we stay here, we're going to burn to death!" Freya said. "So what are we going to do?"

I stood and brushed the leaves from my clothes. "The only thing we can do," I said. "We have to stop the fire."

Freya, Daniel and I sat in the middle of the courtyard, my project spread out on the ground. I pointed at the map.

"From the burn pattern, the fire must have started in one of these three rooms: the science lab, the kitchen or the library," I said. "See? They're all stacked right on top of each other, in the block right next to the bell tower. No one knows *how* the fire started, but they do know *where*."

"So where do *we* start?" Freya said. "The library, the lab or the kitchen?"

"Good question," I said. "Daniel, you know this school better than we do. Any ideas?"

"Well," Daniel said. "I still don't understand why you think there's going to be a fire. But Mr Lamont is fond of science. Always conducting experiments into this new thing called 'electricity'. Have you heard of it?"

"*Electricity?*" Freya raised her eyebrows. "You're joking, right?"

"Load of bunkum," Daniel continued. "Voodoo!" He waggled his fingers in the air.

"Well, actually . . . " Freya began.

I shook my head. "Don't bother," I whispered. It would be far too hard to explain and we didn't have the time. "Daniel," I said, "I think you're on to something. Experiments in electricity sound quite dangerous. And fiery."

"Mr Lamont did burn a hole in his waistcoat on one occasion," Daniel said.

"That settles it." I slammed my folder shut. "To the lab."

We walked up the front steps and back into the school. I felt like I was stepping right into one of my old photos. The corridors were empty of lockers and dim without the fluorescent lighting overhead. The classrooms were just as bleak. No colourful maps hung from the walls. No pet hamsters or aquariums. No computers or television monitors. Just rows of simple wood desks all facing dull blackboards. My legs got twitchy just trying to imagine sitting there all day.

"So what do you do in class?" I asked Daniel.

"Do? Same as you, I assume," he said. "Copy our lines. Write our times tables. Recite the kings of England. The usual lessons."

Yeah, the usual. Suddenly, the twenty-first-century Weirville School didn't sound all that bad. I was about to ask him more, but a man's voice suddenly boomed down the hallway.

"Why isn't every pupil in lessons?"

Daniel's eyes grew wide.

"Mr Lamont!" he whispered. "Quick! If he catches us, we'll be for the birch! We have to hide." Daniel looked up and down the hallway, then raced away in the opposite direction from the voice. We took off after him. He stopped at a set of grand oak doors and shoved them open. "Get inside!" he said.

Freya and I hurried in and stood out of the way

against the wall of an entryway, as Daniel pushed the doors closed.

"What was that all about?" Freya said.

"The headmaster. Mr Lamont," Daniel said. "He's mad. Once caned a pupil for fastening his shirt improperly. The poor chap couldn't sit down for an entire week!"

"Sounds like a great guy," Freya said. She glanced around the darkened entryway. "Where are we now?"

I flipped open my project and scanned the map. Judging from our position, this had to be the . . .

"Library," Daniel said, just as my finger landed on the room.

"Oooooh, the library!" Freya said. "I love libraries! Let's check it out!"

"Hold on, Frey—" I said. The library was one of the

places the fire might have started. We had to be on the lookout.

But, in typical Freya fashion, she had disappeared into the room: Daniel and I had no choice but to go after her.

We stepped from the entryway into a large room with a tall, wood-beamed ceiling that peaked in the centre. Dozens of half-filled bookshelves lined the space, while a huge pile of books was stacked right in the centre of the room, which was sort of odd.

More grey children sat in perfect rows at long tables, mouths moving silently.

They turned the pages of their books. At exactly the same time.

"Wow!" said Freya, coming up to us. "This place is amazing! Our library is so small and rubbish." She went to a corner and started running her fingers along the spines of the books shelved there. "I could spend days in here!" She sighed as she dropped into a nearby chair.

"Me, too," Daniel said, taking a seat next to her. "Mr Lamont is always scolding me for having too much imagination. He believes books are a waste of time." He rolled his eyes. "They're certainly a good deal better than setting your waistcoat on fire, if you ask my opinion."

Freya giggled.

"C'mon, Frey." I scanned the room for potential flammable material. "We don't have time to sit around reading!"

Suddenly, a low chanting came from somewhere deep within the shelves.

Freya spun around. "What was that?" she whispered.

I strained to listen. "I don't know," I said. But, there was something very, very familiar about the tune . . .

"It's 'Happy Birthday'," Freya said, gripping my arm.

CHAPTER 7

Daniel looked at Freya and me clutching each other and laughed.

"Don't worry," he said. "That's just Miss Feynman, the librarian. She's nice."

Yeah, well, I didn't care how nice these nineteenth-century fogies happened to be – this place was still giving me the creeps.

Something rustled behind us. I spun around, fists raised.

A young woman in a floor-length dress and her hair in a bun swooped down on us from behind a bookshelf. I quickly dropped my hands to my sides.

"Hullo, Miss Feynman," Daniel said with a grin. The librarian reached over and ruffled his hair.

"How's my favourite student today?" she said in a sweet, sing-song voice.

"I am very well, ma'am," Daniel said, still grinning like an idiot.

"Glad to hear it, dear," she replied.

"Swot," I muttered.

Daniel shot me a look.

Miss Feynman pulled a handkerchief from her sleeve, sniffled and dabbed her eyes. She gazed miserably at the piles of books.

"Excuse me, miss," Freya said. "Are you OK?"

"Oh, aren't you a dear thing!" Miss Feynman smoothed her hands down the front of her dress and pushed a few loose strands of hair back into place. "Yes, yes, I am fine. Merely the dust. From the shelves."

"Is that why all the books are on the floor?" I asked. "Are you cleaning?"

"Indeed. Just clearing out the, um, *excess.*" She sighed. "Shouldn't you be in lessons with the other boys and girls? You know how Mr Lamont feels about truancy."

Just then she stopped talking and cocked her head to the side. There was a strange *stomp, shuffle* sound coming from somewhere beyond the bookshelves. *Stomp, shuffle. Stomp, shuffle.*

Miss Feynman's face turned pale. Well, even paler than it already was.

"Quickly, children!" she whispered. "Hide yourselves! Mr Lamont will punish you if he finds you here!"

We dodged behind a bookcase just as the headmaster rounded the corner. I peered out from between the books. A large shadow darkened the floor by Miss Feynman's feet. The shadow stood with feet slightly apart, hands on hips, muscular arms bulging.

I recognised that pose from the picture in Mr Malton's study.

"What's going on here?" Mr Lamont said. His voice was a deep growl. "Why aren't these books cleared out yet?"

"Well, I have been working at it, Mr Lamont, sir," the librarian answered. "But the children have been busy reading and . . . "

"*Busy? Reading?* That's a contradiction in terms!" Mr Lamont said with a snort. "It is high time this waste of space was demolished so I can construct a new science laboratory!"

Freya's face screwed up tight. "That's lame," she whispered.

Daniel nodded.

Personally, I felt the whole school could be demolished as a waste of space. But if I had to choose between science and reading, I know which one I'd pick.

"But, Mr Lamont, sir," Miss Feynman said. "The power of stories and books opens the mind. Expands one's horizons. Broadens their—"

"Oh, spare me the drivel," said the head. "Who needs a bunch of fairy tales and wishful thinking when the real world is full of discoveries to explore?

Electricity, phrenology, mesmerism, alchemy, the occult . . . " Mr Lamont's shadow moved closer to the trembling librarian and his finger poked in the air. "I want this place cleaned out. By the end of the day!" He walked towards the door, then turned back. "And then you may pack your things and go, too."

Miss Feynman gasped. "But, sir . . . I will be destitute."

Mr Lamont laughed. "Well, that's not my problem, is it? Perhaps now you will consider dedicating your life to more useful pursuits. Perhaps you might even find a husband, like a proper young lady!"

As soon as his footsteps disappeared, Daniel, Freya and I came out from behind the bookcase.

Freya rolled her eyes. "Of all the outdated, stupid things to say – it's like he's stuck in the nineteenth century!"

91

I didn't bother to point out the obvious.

Miss Feynman stood there shaking silently, hands over her face.

"Don't worry. I'm sure he can't mean it," I said.

Miss Feynman removed her hands from her face and gave a watery smile. "Oh, he most certainly does." She began absent-mindedly pulling books from the shelves and stacking them in piles around her feet.

"I think perhaps he has been sniffing too many of his science potions," Daniel said.

"What will you do now?" asked Freya.

"Do not be concerned," said Miss Feynman, bravely. "Perhaps now I shall fulfil my dream of becoming a headmistress. Then I can be sure no child is ever without a book." She sighed. "All the same, I wish he didn't have to make this announcement today . . . today of *all* days." She sighed again and went back to emptying the shelves.

"There must be something we can do," Freya whispered to me. "She looks so sad. I think she's been crying."

"Can you blame her? Working in a place like this, for a nut-job like Lamont?" I said. "But we don't have time to worry about it." There wasn't much point trying to help a ghost. "We've got to stop that fire!"

We headed for the door.

As I reached for the doorknob, I froze.

My hand! It was ghostly white: like the kids in the pictures; like the ones turning pages at the tables across the room; like those drones marching through the halls. I reached out and touched my skin. It was ice cold. I pulled my hand back, shaking.

93

I was starting to get a horrible feeling about this: a feeling that if we didn't stop the fire, we'd be stuck in that photograph with all the children who'd died.

And that would *really* ruin my night.

CHAPTER 8

In the hallway, I cast a worried glance at my sister. I could've sworn her freckles were disappearing. Her eyes were completely grey now, and the pink in her cheeks was gone.

There was no time to waste.

"Which way to the lab?" I asked Daniel.

He pointed a pale finger towards a dark stairway leading down, at the end of the corridor.

"It's got to be the lab where the fire started,"

Freya said, as we walked quickly down the hall, keeping to the sides and trying not to be seen. "I mean, did you see that Lamont guy? He's a lunatic! '*Books are a waste of space …*!'" she muttered. "Whatever!"

"Excuse me!" a voice said from behind.

We spun around to see the prefect who'd locked us in the bell tower, mouth drawn in a thin line. "Why, precisely, are you three miscreants out here roaming the school?"

"We, uh …" Freya started. The prefect looked up and down the hall, then leaned forward. His breath felt like an icy frost creeping across my face. I rocked back on my heels.

"How did you get out of the tower?"

"We did what you asked, so we left." I smiled, pulled a piece of paper from the pocket in my blazer and

unfolded it under the prefect's nose. He squinted at my line – I will not run in the corridor, nor disregard the school uniform, nor disobey the school rules ... a million times – and huffed.

"Well, aren't you clever?" he said.

I shrugged and jammed the paper back inside my blazer.

"Very well," the prefect said. "You cheated your way out of the tower, but now we'll see how well you do in ... physical education." He grinned malevolently.

Freya, Daniel and I looked at each other and, without a word, took off in the other direction. The prefect shouted after us, but we ignored him. We ran. And ran. Until we couldn't hear his shouts any more.

"I think ... we lost ... him," Daniel said, panting.

"That was enough physical education for me!" Freya leaned back against the corridor wall.

I stopped and rested my hands on my knees, catching my breath. "Nice job, guys—"

And, just like that, the prefect was standing in front of us, sneering, his big, creepy eyes unblinking. My heart nearly popped out of my chest.

"How did he—?"

The prefect grabbed Freya and me by the arm. "How many times do I have to tell you? There's no running in the halls!"

"Ow!" Freya yelled.

I tried to wriggle myself away, but the prefect kept a death-grip on me.

"OK, OK," I said, leaning sideways and swatting at the prefect's hand. "Physical education time."

"You, too," the prefect said to Daniel.

We were hauled to the gymnasium. I really didn't want to waste any more time, but at least it was PE – the one subject in school I'm actually good at. It certainly had to beat being locked up in a bell tower.

We stopped at the gymnasium door and the prefect swung it open. But instead of the usual trainer-squeaking, yells and high fives, the room was filled with rows of more drone-like children, in white vests and shorts. They were taking turns to run through some sort of obstacle course, moving with perfect precision – vaulting the horse, walking the balance beam and climbing the ropes that dangled from the high ceiling.

Suddenly, a skinny boy slipped from halfway up a rope and hit the floor. He pulled himself up on his elbows and glanced nervously around.

Mr Lamont emerged from behind a stack of mats

and stood over the trembling boy, like a lion over a wounded gazelle. "Get up!" he yelled. "Use your arms and your legs! There is no reward for failure!"

The boy nodded and climbed, wincing, to his feet. He gripped the rope again and began shimmying up.

Mr Lamont scanned the room, presumably in search of more failure to correct. His eyes landed on us. "You over there!" he said. As he moved in our direction, I noticed he walked with a slight limp, stepping heavily on his left foot and dragging his right. *Stomp, shuffle. Stomp, shuffle.*

"What's the matter with his leg?" I whispered to Daniel.

"Stricken by the devil as a child," Daniel said. "They say his whole village was afflicted. Mr Lamont" – Daniel gulped – "was the lone survivor."

"Oh," I said.

Freya groaned. "Per-lease," she said. "It's more likely to be polio, don't you think?" Daniel looked at her questioningly. All in all, I felt, he was dealing with our twenty-first-centuryness pretty well. But Freya's geek knowledge really wasn't helping.

Mr Lamont got closer. He was much larger in real life than he was in his pictures – tall with broad shoulders, wire-rimmed glasses perched on his prominent nose. He wore a blazer and tie and was monochrome like the students. But his eyes were twin, soulless dots of pitch black.

"Yeah," I muttered. "I think I'll stick with the devil theory."

Mr Lamont stopped in front of us and crossed his arms, which was a struggle, because they were bulging like balloons. "I will not abide tardiness!" he said.

The prefect shoved Freya, Daniel and me forward. "I found these troublemakers out roaming the hallways."

"Is that so?" the headmaster said.

Daniel shifted nervously. Freya dug her fingers into my arm. I had to do something.

"I'm sorry, sir," I said. "I think there's been a mistake. We weren't roaming the hallways. We were just heading to the science laboratory and got lost."

"Mistake?" Mr Lamont said. "Your mistake was not attending physical education on time as required."

"I know, sir, but you see—" I said.

"A healthy body equals a healthy mind!" the headmaster said.

"We're worried that—"

"And since you seem so keen to speak on behalf of your friends here, perhaps you would like to represent them in the assault course, as well?" Mr Lamont pointed towards the clock on the gymnasium wall. "You have until the clock strikes twelve to complete it." He bent down and put his face only a few inches from mine. "Or your hides will be caned bloody."

"But sir," I said. "That's only two minutes! There's no way!"

Behind us, the heavy gymnasium doors banged shut. A latch dropped over the handles. Something told me there was no getting back out. Not without playing the headmaster's impossible game.

And winning.

Mr Lamont raised his hand in the air. "Make that one minute, fifty-five seconds."

I yanked off my blazer, threw it to the ground and took off running, rudely barging the drone-kid whose turn it was out of the way. I vaulted the horse and scrambled down the narrow mats. I was barely halfway across them when there was a *whoosh* overhead, and something slammed into the pile of mats, making them tremble. A heavy leather ball! Another flew in front of me, hitting the wall with a slap. Then another ... they were coming out of nowhere, hard and fast. I dodged as fast as I could, but they kept coming.

"Hey! That's not fair!" I shouted. In reply, one caught me right in the stomach, knocking the wind out of me. I tumbled to the mat, gasping for breath.

"One minute, fifteen seconds," Mr Lamont said from the starting line.

"Come on, Brendan!" yelled Freya.

I clambered back to my feet, still struggling for air, and hurried to the balance beam. There was no step, so I reached up with both hands and hoisted myself onto the bar. As soon as I did, the thing seemed to rise higher. And higher.

I looked down and my legs trembled. I had to be at least four metres in the air; the wooden gym floor lay far below.

The drone-like children now stood along the gymnasium wall, unblinking eyes following my every move – the assault course was bad enough; why did those kids have to keep watching me like that? And with a sudden swoop in my stomach I realised – *they could see me*. When we'd first arrived in their freaky school, the only ones who saw us were Daniel and that prefect. Did it mean that I – Freya and I – were becoming more like them?

I sucked in a breath, told myself to concentrate and moved slowly forward. The beam was barely wider than my foot. I wobbled and held my arms out for balance. Sweat began to trickle down the back of my neck. I glanced at the clock. Less than a minute to go. I was never going to make it. I looked at my sister and Daniel, watching me with wide eyes.

I couldn't give up. I had to do this.

Legs still shaking, I stuck one foot in front of the other, somehow managing to make it to the end of the beam. But how was I supposed to get off this thing? If I jumped, I'd probably break my leg – or worse, crack my skull in half.

Straight ahead, the climbing ropes dangled and twisted in the air. One creaked back and forth in my direction. Maybe if I could just grab it, I'd be able to climb down it. I teetered on my right foot and reached out.

The rope shot forward. *Yes!* But instead of landing in my hand, the thing snaked itself around my ankle,

flipping me upside down with a jolt. I dangled helplessly in the air, swinging back and forth over the
balance beam. I gripped the beam with both hands,
straining all my muscles to pull myself down flat. The
rope pulled back, yanking me backwards as my fin-
gernails clawed the sides of the beam. I struggled and
thrashed my legs.

"Let! Me! Go!"

The rope tightened – and then suddenly I was
released.

I fell onto the beam, sat up and gasped for breath.
Then yelled as the beam plunged down towards the
gym floor, where it thankfully halted at its normal
height. Once I was sure it had stopped, I allowed
myself another shaky breath before I started to swing
my leg over it to dismount. As I did so, the hairs on
the back of my neck began to prickle: this was easy.

Too easy. I looked around just in time to see the rope swinging at me again – this time, twisted in the shape of a hangman's noose. I tried to scramble backwards, but the thing was coming at me way too fast.

"Noooo!" I yelled, as the noose slipped over my head. The rope tightened. I grabbed at my neck. "Help!" I choked out.

Freya and Daniel ran alongside the beam, reached up and swatted at the rope. It twisted back and forth, pulling me along with it. I gripped the beam with my legs. If I fell off, I'd be hanged for certain.

I had to create a bit of slack somehow or I was going to suffocate.

Shakily, I managed to stand up on the beam and, as I did so, the rope loosened for just a moment. I quickly slipped it back over my head, held on to the noose and swung down. I hit the floor with a thud and fell to my knees.

Freya and Daniel rushed to my side. Each grabbed an arm, helping me to my feet.

"Are you OK?" Freya said.

"Yeah." I looked at the clock. Only twenty-five seconds to go. "But there's no way I'm going to make it," I said. "We've got to do something to stop the time!"

Mr Lamont was marching up and down in front of the black and white children, flicking their chins, ordering them to stand up straighter. A crack of thunder sounded and lightning flashed through the hall.

"I know!" I said. "Freya, you distract Mr Lamont. Daniel, you wind back the clock!"

Freya nodded then ran over to the headmaster. I

reached for a climbing rope and began to shimmy up it. As I did, I could hear my sister playing her part.

"Mr Lamont, sir," she said, in her best I'm-so-confused-please-help-me voice. "You know about electricity."

That got his attention. He turned to face her, head cocked, ready to listen.

"Ummm," Freya said, "does lightning come up from the ground or down from the sky?"

"Well, yes, electricity can be a bit confusing. Especially for a girl," Mr Lamont started.

I could just picture the steam streaming out of Freya's ears. "Oh, really?" she said. "Perhaps you could enlighten me on electrostatic energy, then. I've always wondered how much is needed to create one lightning bolt?"

"You have?" Mr Lamont said. "Well, certainly, let me explain ... "

Out of the corner of my eye, I saw Daniel standing on a chair, pushing the clock's minute hand back.

"... the current is exceptionally strong ... enough to kill a man ... "

Daniel clambered down just as I reached the top of the rope.

Mr Lamont suddenly stopped talking and searched the room. "Wait!" he said. "What has become of that friend of yours?"

His eyes landed on me, then the clock. The minute hand twitched to twelve – just as I leapt from the rope and crossed the finish line.

The gymnasium door flew open with a bang. A gust of cold wind blew into the room and seemed to freeze Mr Lamont in place. The room grew darker.

The line of children shimmered dimly against the wall.

"Let's go!" I yelled to Freya and Daniel.

We scrambled towards the door. I stopped on the way out to grab my dusty blazer from the floor. I felt for my project. It was still safely tucked inside.

Now to get to the science lab and stop the fire.

CHAPTER 9

I breathed a sigh of relief when we made it into the corridor with no one following us.

"That was messed up," I said.

"I know, right?" Freya pulled her bag of pick'n'mix from her pocket and started chomping away. I studied her face and my heart sank.

Her freckles had vanished completely.

"We need to hurry," I said. "Daniel, which way to the lab?"

He pointed down the hall just as a line of students shuffled past, eyes straight ahead, completely drained of colour. They didn't smile, turn their heads or even blink.

It was only a matter of time before we ended up just like them. Maybe we already had ...

The children filed into a classroom.

"OK," I said. "Let's do this."

Daniel led us downstairs to a thick wooden door marked "Laboratory for Scientific Studies". I peered through the crack left by the slightly open door. Mr Lamont stood at the front of the class, instructing rows of monochrome students who were scratching out notes in unison on their slates.

"How did he get here so fast?" I said, amazed. "Has he found some way to bypass the space–time continuum or something?"

"The what?" Daniel said.

"Never mind."

"Shhhh!" Freya put her finger to her lips and pushed the door open slowly.

"There are some empty seats towards the back," Daniel whispered. "If we keep silent, he may not notice us."

But the minute we stepped into the room, Mr Lamont looked up from his lectern and narrowed his eyes. "What is the meaning of this? How dare you join a class halfway through?" he said. The students stopped writing, hands frozen mid-air.

I cleared my throat. "We came straight from the gymnasium, sir," I said. I thought he should have known that. But he just stared, as if seeing us for the very first time.

Freya piped up. "Yes, we stayed late, sir. Healthy bodies create healthy minds."

Mr Lamont pursed his lips. His right eyelid twitched. I supposed he couldn't argue with his own motto. Instead, he focused his black-eyed gaze on me.

"Why is your blazer so dirty?" he said. "Have you no respect?"

I smoothed down my jacket and dust puffed from the lapels. Must have been that tumble I took in the bell tower. "Sorry, sir," I mumbled.

"And when was the last time you had a haircut?" he continued.

Hey! Now that was rude! I mean, that guy was one to talk – his hair looked like it had been sheared by an out-of-control hedge trimmer.

"I'm watching you," he said. "Now take your seats!"

I slipped into an empty chair. Daniel and Freya sat behind me.

I shifted around on the hard wood of the seat, inspecting the room. It wasn't nearly as empty as the other classrooms we'd walked passed; in fact, it was stuffed full with all kinds of strange boxes and containers. I looked a little closer at a row of glass jars along the wall. In the first one, an eyeball bounced around in some sort of gel-like liquid. Gross! But it was even grosser when it started staring right back at me.

My eyes flicked to the next jar. This one held what appeared to be a heart – still beating. A bit further on, what I could have sworn was a shrunken human head – stringy mop of hair and all – floated in more strange liquid. I choked back a gag and leaned towards the boy next to me.

"Is that what I think it is?" I pointed at the head.

The boy said nothing. He just kept scraping the chalk over his slate in time with the rest of the class, eyes trained on Mr Lamont.

The headmaster cleared his throat and glared at me. I sat up straight.

"As I was saying," Mr Lamont continued. "Experiments in electricity are still in their infancy." The thunder boomed outside. Mr Lamont looked towards the window with a wicked grin. "But we have come a long way since Benjamin Franklin tied a key to a kite in a lightning storm." He rubbed his hands together. "Let me show you just how far ... "

The headmaster went to a cupboard and carefully pulled out a trolley that held a circuit board covered with dials, wires and switches. He adjusted his glasses and twisted one of the large knobs. The board sparked.

"I plan to take it a stage further than Mr Franklin!" – Mr Lamont had to yell over the buzzing machine – "and harness the power of electricity for even greater benefits!" He cranked the dial full throttle.

Sparks flew higher, sizzling and cracking in the air. My hands gripped the old wood of the desk.

This must be how the fire started!

"Mr Lamont!" – I jumped from my seat – "Stop!"

The headmaster paused, twisted the dial again to turn the current down and looked at me with irritation. "Excuse me? How dare you—?"

"I mean, let me help you!" I said.

"Swot," Daniel said, under his breath.

I had to laugh. "Shut up," I whispered over my shoulder as I raced to the front of the class.

"Mr Lamont, sir!" I continued. "I was just hoping

you'd show me how this exciting machine works." I reached out to touch a knob.

Mr Lamont swatted my hand away. "That is precisely what I *was* doing," he said. "Now return to your seat at once!"

My mind raced. I had to distract him somehow and dismantle the thing. I shot a look at Freya and pointed toward the circuit board mouthing, "Do something!"

Freya wrinkled her nose and sat there for a moment. Then her eyes opened wide and she nodded. With a flourish, she swung her arm and knocked the slate from her desk. It clattered to the floor.

Mr Lamont exhaled loudly and searched the classroom. "I don't know …" he said irritably. "These constant interruptions!"

"Sorry, sir!" Freya said. "I'm just a girl, you know. I get a little overwhelmed by science!" She scrambled to

the floor to pick up her chalk and slate, in the process knocking down her chair. It crashed into Daniel's desk, sending his slate flying. "Oh, no!" Freya cried. "Now I've really done it!" She glanced in my direction and glared.

I'd have to make up to her for humiliating herself later.

In that moment, I seized the opportunity to grab the circuit board and heave it into the air. With a grunt, I smashed it back down on the trolley. The thing cracked into pieces. Knobs and dials rolled across the floor. Coils sprang across the room. Sparks sputtered – and then stopped.

Mr Lamont spun back to me.

"What have you done?" The look on his face was more like I'd harmed his first-born baby, rather than broken a piece of equipment. "You ... you ... idiot!"

he yelled, his eyes popping at the sight of his beloved circuit board, scattered in bits on the floor. His whole body shook with rage and he grabbed me by the blazer.

Right about then was normally when I'd crack a joke and the class would burst out laughing. But not this time. The room was eerily silent. And my legs were trembling so hard I reckoned it was only Mr Lamont's fierce grip keeping me upright.

"You will pay for this!" he spat.

I screwed my eyes shut, hoping that I'd just stopped the fire and that when I opened them again, I'd be home.

CHAPTER 10

I counted to three and opened my eyes. Mr Lamont still had hold of my blazer. He sucked in a deep breath.

"What do you have to say for yourself?" he said.

"I didn't do it?" I said slowly. I wasn't even convincing myself.

"You mean to tell me my circuit board simply leapt to the ground and disintegrated all on its own?" Mr Lamont squeezed my blazer tightly around me.

"No, sir!" I sputtered. "It must've been the awesome power of electricity!"

"Are you trying to be funny?"

"Not at all, sir," I said. And for once, I wasn't.

Mr Lamont released his grip and I wobbled backwards. He glanced around the room. All of the students sat stony-faced, except Daniel and Freya. Daniel's eyes were wide with alarm and Freya had a death-grip on her desk.

"Well, yes. Electricity is rather 'awesome', I suppose." Mr Lamont looked thoughtful for a moment. "But I've had my fill of your antics. Three whacks with Thrasher ought to adjust your attitude."

Just then, a loud clanging reverberated through the lab. The bell! The students rose silently from their desks and began marching single-file towards the door.

Now was my chance.

I darted over to join the row of kids and looked back over my shoulder. "Sorry, sir!" I called in Mr Lamont's direction. "Can't be late! I know how you can't abide tardiness!" I hurried out before the head-master had a chance to grab me. Freya and Daniel caught up with me in the hallway.

As we walked past a row of windows, Freya leaned towards me and whispered in my ear, "What are we still doing here? I thought once we stopped the fire we'd be able to go home!"

I peered outside. The mist still hung low over the school grounds. The gate remained shut.

"Maybe we haven't actually stopped it yet," I said.

The line of students rounded the corner and marched up the stairs.

"Where's everyone going now?" I asked Daniel.

"Refectory," he said. "For lunch." He made a gagging noise and wrapped his hands around his neck. "If you can call it that."

Freya laughed. "Has anyone ever told you that you look a lot like the lead singer of Side Street?" she said.

I rolled my eyes.

"The what of whom?" Daniel said.

"Oh, yeah, right," Freya said. "Guess you wouldn't have heard of them in 1863. They're just like the, you know, cutest boy band ever." She sighed.

I didn't think it was possible, but I'm pretty sure Daniel's ghost-white skin turned pink for a moment. I rolled my eyes again.

"C'mon, guys," I said. "We still have a fire to stop. Which way to the kitchen?"

"This way," Daniel said. He pulled us from the line

126

of students filing into the dining hall and directed us to a large, dark, cave-like room right next door.

A large butcher's block sat in the centre of the room on a table, covered with what appeared to be animal bones, feathers and traces of blood. I tried not to puke. Against the wall to our right, on a long, filthy stove, rows of pots boiled over with foul-looking stews. A thick-set woman wearing a tattered mob cap stood with her back to us, scratching one armpit vigorously with a potato masher.

"Who's that?" Freya asked.

"Cook," Daniel whispered. "She's crazy. Best she doesn't see us here!"

We ducked beneath the table. Spoons rattled and banged. Cook sang off-key as she lumbered across the dirty floor, picked out some rotten-looking vegetables from a sack and tossed them into a pot.

"Three blind mice,

Three blind mice.

See how they run!

See how they run!

They all ran after the farmer's wife

Who cut off their tails with a carving knife!"

The cook cackled.

A large rat scurried towards us and skidded to a stop inches from my face. I swear it actually looked terrified. I wanted to shout out to the poor thing, but Cook's meaty hand suddenly swooped down and grabbed the rodent by the tail. I heard something slap down on the butcher's block above us, followed by a screech, quickly silenced by the thump of the cleaver.

Gross.

"Have you ever seen such a thing in your life?" Cook

128

warbled as she chucked the headless rat into a bubbling pot of stew.

"Ewwww!" Freya's hand flew over her mouth and she suppressed a retch.

"This is actually one of Cook's better meals," Daniel whispered. "You don't want to try her Monday special – blood pudding is even worse than it sounds."

I would have laughed, but I was pretty sure he wasn't joking. He tugged my sleeve.

"We need to get out of here," he said. "Before she spots us and makes us eat her stew. Or worse, puts us in it!"

"But this could be where the fire started," I said. "We need to have a quick look around."

We slid from beneath the table and, crouching over, moved stealthily along another dark wall. Dirty

mixing bowls lined the shelf above us. Freya reached up for one and sniffed it.

"Mmmmm," she said. "This one actually smells good. Like cake!"

"Cake?" Daniel said. "Cook would never make anything that nice."

"Really?" Freya stuck her finger in and gave it a lick. "Tastes like cake to me."

"Freya!" I hissed. "Are you mad? Look at this place. That stuff could be made from sewage for all you know!"

Freya just shrugged. "It's pretty good."

I was about to debate the finer points of eating out of random bowls in haunted schools when Cook spun around.

"Who's in my kitchen?" she said.

We ducked behind another oven. Cook's footsteps

130

pounded in our direction, then came to a sudden stop. I looked at Freya and Daniel, eyebrows raised.

"Is she gone?" I whispered.

"Aha!" Cook yelled, leaping at us, bloodied meat cleaver raised once more over her head. "There you are! Second time my cooking's been interrupted today. I'm not having it!"

I jumped. Daniel squeaked. Freya dropped the cake bowl and it clattered away across the floor. Cook leaned down and peered at us from her watery left eye; the right one was hidden beneath a shabby leather eye patch.

"Keen to eat, are you?" she said with an evil grin, exposing a row of snaggly yellow teeth.

As if!

"What, cat got your tongue?" she said. "Very well then, since you're here, I'll just have to make you

my official food tasters!" She grabbed my collar with the same incredible strength as the prefect and Mr Lamont and dragged me over to the bubbling pots.

The smell was atrocious. Worse than the time Freya had tried to cook mud pies – worms and all – on our kitchen stove. I held my breath.

Cook laughed and pushed me face-first towards a large black cauldron. Flames licked the sides, popping and crackling. The woman grabbed a mouldy wooden spoon and began to stir her evil concoction. As she did so, her grimy apron dangled precariously close to the fire. I could see burn marks all along the edges of the fabric. A puff of smoke twisted into the air – the fire was getting bigger by the second.

This had to be it – this must have been how the school burned down!

"Wait! Stop!" I said. "I don't think that's safe!"

"I don't think it tastes too good, either," Freya muttered, behind me.

"What was that?" Cook looked over her shoulder at Freya with her one good eye as she twirled the spoon. A half-dozen eyeballs floated to the surface of the stew, and I wondered with a shudder if one belonged to Cook.

"This is a fire hazard," I said.

Cook ignored me and scooped up some of the fetid mixture. "I'm still working on the recipe, so you need to smile and say you love it ... " Her voice growled. "Or else, you'll keep tasting until it's right!"

She held out the spoon. A couple of drops splattered on the ground, and the floor sizzled as if burned by acid.

OK, I can do this, I thought, reminding myself of

the time in the first year when I was dared to eat a spoonful of Pet Munch dog food. I closed my eyes, leaned in and took a sip from Cook's spoon.

As soon as the mixture hit my taste buds I felt my whole stomach flip over: it was like the canal on a warm day, the smell from the sewers and my dad's breath after a night out with "the lads" – all rolled into one. I swallowed hard.

"Lovely!" I smiled. "Yum!"

Cook unleashed her snaggle-toothed grin and extended the spoon to Freya.

I gave her a "good luck" nod. Freya leaned forward cautiously and sucked down a mouthful. Instantly, her hands flew to her throat. She swayed on her feet, choking. The colour – what was left of it – drained completely from her face.

"Freya!" I yelled.

She made a strange gagging sound and finally fell to the floor. I'd seen that look on her face before. *Peanuts!* If I didn't do something fast, Freya was going to die.

CHAPTER 11

I grabbed Freya by the jacket and tried to pull her up. Her head lolled back and her eyes stayed closed. Cook looked at her, then peered into the boiling vat, sniffed and rubbed the back of her hand under her bulbous nose.

"Hmm ... maybe too much salt," she said. "Or maybe it was those mushrooms I found growing on the lavatory floor ... "

"You've killed my sister!" I shouted at her. I was too angry to be scared.

Daniel looked down at Freya, then back at me with alarm. "Is she OK?" he said. "What's happening?"

"Cook! How many peanuts did you put in the stew?" I shouted again. But she wasn't listening; instead, she was making notes on her recipe book.

Daniel's eyebrows arched. "'Peanuts'? What is a 'peanut'?"

I gave Freya another shake. Her face was slack. This had to be the worst day of my life. Tears began to well up in my eyes. OK, so she could be a total nightmare but, still, she was my sister, and I didn't know what I'd do if something happened to her. I stroked her cheek.

"C'mon, Frey!" I said. "Please be OK. I'll stop calling you Fraidy-cat!" My sister stayed limp. "I'll do anything! Anything!" I choked back a sob. "I'll even definitely take you to that stupid Side Street concert! I *promise!*"

At that, Freya lifted her head a bit, opened one eye and grinned at me.

"What?" I couldn't believe it. "Of all the dirty tricks!" I said, not sure whether to be annoyed or relieved.

"Shhhh!" Freya shook her head and nodded towards the bubbling pot.

I glanced around the kitchen. Not a jar of peanut butter in sight. Of course! Daniel didn't know what a peanut was because they didn't have peanuts here back in 1863. Freya dropped her head back down. Now I got it – she was giving me time to put out the fire!

Cook rattled cans and jars on a low shelf. Something toppled off and smashed to the floor,

sending a putrid cloud up in the air. "Where *is* my cod liver oil?" she said with a snort. "That ought to wake the girl up ..."

I had to hurry. I slipped behind Cook, who was still rifling through jars. The flames were shooting higher around the cauldron of rancid stew, inching closer to an overflowing vat of oil on the shelf above. One more minute and the whole place would ignite.

I searched frantically for something to put out the fire. Yeah, too much to ask for a fire extinguisher. No bucket of water in sight, either. Well, there was only one thing to do.

I grabbed a suspiciously slimy oven cloth and tried to lift the pot by its handles, but it was too heavy – wouldn't budge an inch. What did Cook put in there? Stones?

"Psst!" I whispered. "Daniel! Help me!"

Daniel hurried over and grabbed the handle, sloshing stew all over my blazer.

"Sorry," he said.

"No worries. On three," I said. "One ... two ... three ... "

With a grunt, we heaved the pot and dumped the bubbling liquid over the flames. The foul ingredients sizzled and burned: an eyeball popped, rat hair singed, what looked like a piece of shoe leather turned black and shrivelled. I realised that we weren't just saving the kids of 1863 from a fire; we were saving them from their *lunch*. I held my breath. The fire sputtered, crackled ...

And then went out.

Yes!

Daniel and I dropped the pot. I raised my hand for a high five.

"Nice work, mate!" My hand hovered in the air. Daniel shot me a bewildered look, then lifted his right arm and saluted.

I chuckled. Good thing I hadn't tried to fist-bump him – he might have punched me.

A shriek came from the other side of the room. We spun around to see Cook standing with her hands tugging frantically at her mob cap. "My stew!" she bellowed. "What have you little imbeciles done to my stew?"

She raised the meat cleaver above her head and lumbered in our direction.

Great, averted the fire, only to die at the hands of a psychotic chef.

"C'mon!" I yelled. "Let's get out of here!"

"Don't have to ask me twice!" Freya jumped up and the three of us scrambled towards the door, knocking

down pots, pans and jars of what looked like pickled hooves as we went, in an attempt to slow the cook down. But she clomped right through the mess, cleaver swinging, bloodied apron swooshing.

"Get back here!" she yelled. "You have to help me make a whole new stew – a tasty little dish I like to call 'Pupil Surprise'. And you're the most important ingredient!" She cackled shrilly.

The woman was barking mad. And fast, too! She skidded around the butcher's block, blocking our escape to the door, and caught the corner of Freya's blazer.

I slowed and scanned a shelf, grabbing a jar of pepper. "Looking for this?" I said, tossing a handful towards her face.

Cook coughed and sputtered and rubbed her one good eye, giving us just enough time for Freya to escape her grasp. But we were trapped – Cook may have been blind as she stood sneezing and snorting from the pepper, but she was still standing in the doorway.

We ran back across the kitchen. In my desperation, I spotted a cupboard cleverly hidden in the wall – all I saw was its lock, and a small handle next to that for opening it.

"Quick!" I said. "In here!"

Freya, Daniel and I dived inside. I slammed the door shut, trapping us in complete darkness. Cook's voice echoed through the cavernous room.

"Where are you now, you little terrors?" she said. "You'll be sorry when I find you!" Pots banged and crashed. Cabinets slammed open and shut. Cook's footsteps got closer. My heart pounded in my ears as I waited for her to fling open the cupboard door.

But she continued past, bawling obscenities and threatening to turn us into pies when she finally caught us.

Freya sighed. "Phew," she said. "We did it. The fire is out."

"Yeah," I said. "That's pretty awesome. We've saved everyone."

That's what I hoped, anyway. Once again, we hadn't magically gone home, but at least now we could work out a way to get home without having to worry about being burned to a crisp.

Daniel cleared his throat. "Perhaps now you can explain about this fire you say we've stopped?"

"Later," I said. "Right now, we have to work out how to get out of this kitchen and also . . . get home!" I took a deep breath. Then another. I smelled something. It actually smelled . . . *good*. Definitely not my stinking blazer. Definitely not Cook's cooking. Maybe I was just hallucinating from whatever that madwoman had put in her stew.

"Do you smell that?" I said.

"Yeah," Freya said. I heard her sniff. "It smells like that amazing cake. And I'm starving!"

"That really doesn't make sense," Daniel said. "As I said, Cook would rather smile and dance in her petticoats before she'd ever bake a cake."

Freya snorted. I cracked the cupboard door open a centimetre, letting in a narrow slant of light, and searched for something to get a better look around. A lantern hung on the wall behind me. I plucked it off and ran my hands across the base, feeling for the on switch.

Right. This was 1863. There was no switch.

"Hey, guys," I said. "I need some matches."

"You need some what?" Daniel asked.

"Matches," I said. "To light this."

Daniel shrugged and picked a metal contraption off the shelf. "Here," he said.

I took the thing from his hands and squinted at it in the dim light. A tinderbox. I'd seen one before – in a museum.

"How does this work?" I said.

Daniel looked at me like I was completely daft. "Just put the flint in here and push this." He scraped the metal together.

"Are you two nuts?" Freya exclaimed. "We've just stopped a fire ... let's not start another one!"

"Oh, chill out," I said. The flint caught a spark and I lit the lantern. Now we could see everything in the cupboard, including cobwebs, mouse carcasses – and a new box of candles for a birthday cake. I grabbed the box and shook it. One remaining candle rattled inside.

Wait … the cake batter … the sweet smell … the candles … and what was it the cook had said? "*Second time my cooking's been interrupted today …*"

That's when it hit me.

"The librarian!" I said.

"Miss Feynman?" Daniel asked. "What about her?"

"Remember what she said earlier – 'Today of all days'?" I said.

"So?" Freya shrugged. "She was having a pretty bad day."

"Even worse than you think," I said. "It's her birthday!"

"How sweet," Freya said. "I don't think that's going to help us, though. Not unless she can wish us out of here."

"No, stupid!" I said. "Think about it! The singing. The cake. The candles. All those dry books in the library . . ."

Daniel's eyes grew wide. "You mean *she*'s going to start the fire?"

Freya looked back and forth between us. "Then we haven't stopped it yet!"

I blew out the lantern, opened the cupboard door and peeked outside. I swore I could hear the faint sounds of "Happy Birthday" coming from somewhere up above.

"Let's go," I said. "I have a nasty feeling we don't have much time!"

CHAPTER 12

Thankfully, Cook was still nowhere to be seen so we raced out of the kitchen and down the hallway. We finally reached where the library should have been but, somehow, its doors seemed to fade further from view the faster we ran; we picked up the pace and the corridor grew even longer. Darker. And colder.

"What's going on?" Freya cried.

"I don't know!" I said. "But we have to hurry!"

We ran as fast as our legs could take us, yet the

library doors continued to recede into the distance until they vanished completely.

Daniel huffed and puffed. "I don't know how much faster I can run!" he said.

Suddenly, Freya stopped. "Wait! That's it!" she said with a pant. "No ... running ... "

"What?" Daniel stopped next to her, doubling over. "But if we don't get there, the school will burn down!"

"No," Freya said. "I mean there's *no running in the halls!*"

"Guys!" I said. "This is hardly the time to become swots!"

Daniel blinked a couple of times. "No, Freya's spot on!" he said. "Running in the corridors is against the rules. We must walk."

Freya nodded. "Trust me!" she said.

I stared down the endless hallway. What other choice did I have?

"Right," I said. "We walk."

I had to hold back every urge to bolt down the corridor. Freya, Daniel and I linked arms. One foot in front of the other ... With each measured step, the library came closer.

Finally, we reached the heavy oak doors.

"Who knew they took rules so seriously in the past," I said, and yanked the handle.

The door didn't budge an inch.

But that wasn't the worst of it. An eerie – yet familiar – sound filled the air, sending a chill up my spine. The words were being sung with a manic edge, ratcheting higher and higher, faster and faster, shrill enough to crack glass.

"Oh, no!" I cried. "I think we're too late!"

Daniel jumped in front of me and banged on the door. "Miss Feynman!" he yelled. "Please, open up!"

The singing just got louder, the words less recognisable, muffled by the sound of sobs.

"Miss Feynman!" Daniel yelled again, slumping against the door.

"What are we going to do?" Freya said.

I rubbed my head. I couldn't believe we'd made it this far: getting out of the bell tower, finishing the obstacle course, escaping a crazed cook, outsmarting Mr Lamont ... just to be stopped by a locked door. A stupid locked door.

Wait ... a locked door!

"Hold on!" I scrabbled in my pocket and pulled out the note and key.

You might find this useful.

It *had* to work this time. A faint glimpse of recognition crossed Daniel's face. Without a word, he snatched the key from my hand and slipped it into the lock. With a click, the door slipped open. *Yes!*

We burst inside.

It took a moment for my eyes to adjust. The room was pitch black, except for a flickering glow of light at its centre. I squinted into the darkness. Miss Feynman sat alone at a table, hunched over a birthday cake. The candles cast a strange light across her tear-streaked face. All of the shelves were now empty, the books heaped in piles around her feet.

The librarian wiped her face, took a deep breath and leaned in, preparing to blow. Her long hair fell loose from its bun, dangling closer and closer to the flames. She didn't seem to notice. Smoke curled into the air around her head.

"Miss Feynman!" I said. "Stop!"

The librarian looked up with surprise. "What? Who? Mr Lamont? I'm going, sir!" She leapt up from the chair, shaking, and caught her knee on the table. The cake flew sideways – flaming candles and all – and came crashing down on a pile of books.

With a whoosh, the dusty books burst into flames.

The fire twisted upwards, crackling and popping, shooting sparks across the wooden floor. The room glowed orange and red. Miss Feynman fell back in shock and slumped in the chair, small hands trembling over her face. A flaming book toppled from the pile.

"Noooo!" I ran over and stamped it out with my foot, but it wasn't enough. The pile of books began to burn quickly, flames snaking upwards, licking the tall ceiling. The stack teetered ominously.

Freya ran to my side and helped kick away unlit books. "We're going to die!" she yelled.

"No, we are not!" Daniel said.

While Freya and I stamped on smouldering books, he dashed across the room and grabbed a large cleaner's bucket, tossing away the mop it contained. Water sloshed from the sides as he ran back to the blaze. With a grunt, he heaved the dirty water on the pyre. There was an almighty splash and a *hiss*. Books smoked and sizzled as the fire went out. One last ember popped at the very top of the smoking books and fell to the floor, igniting a copy of *Modern Science*.

"Oh, no, you don't!" I whipped off my blazer and tossed it down, smothering the last of the flames. I waved away the smoke and coughed.

Freya threw her arms around me, and then Daniel.

155

"We did it!" she said. "We stopped the fire!" She planted a kiss right on his cheek.

Daniel definitely blushed this time. Well, if a ghost can blush, I suppose. He cleared his throat and mumbled something. Freya grinned. I smiled with satisfaction and looked at my smouldering jacket.

Oh, no! My project!

I reached over and grabbed the blazer by the sleeve, shaking away the soot. Trembling, I pulled the folder from the inside pocket and checked it. *Phew!* The thing was still intact. I flipped through the pages. Only the edges had burned, but it actually gave the whole report a cool, olde-worlde feel. Awesome. This was A-plus material, for sure.

Miss Feynman stood up shakily and rubbed her red eyes. "Thank you, dear children. I'm not really sure what happened ..." She surveyed the wreckage. "Oh, my books," she said. Her shoulders slumped.

"Cheer up," I said. "It's your birthday, remember?"

"Yeah! Go ahead and make a wish!" Freya added, with a smile.

"A wish. How I long for a wish," Miss Feynman said.

Stomp, shuffle. Stomp, shuffle.

The coldest chill I'd felt all night blew into the room. Miss Feynman wrapped her arms around herself and began shaking again. "Children, go!" she said, urgently.

I followed the path of her wide-eyed stare to the doorway.

"Why do I smell smoke?" boomed Mr Lamont's voice. "Is something burning in here?"

Stomp, shuffle. Stomp, shuffle.

Daniel dodged behind a bookcase, but Freya and I

weren't quite so lucky. We stood there, frozen in place, as Mr Lamont closed in. His black eyes darted between Freya and me.

"You two!" he yelled. "Explain yourselves!"

"Sir," Miss Feynman said, voice quivering. "Please. These children just saved the school. They put out the fire."

"Fire?" Mr Lamont scoffed. "You'd be doing us all a *favour* in burning down this room, full of such claptrap and nonsense as it is!" He glared at Miss Feynman. "And I thought I told you to be out of here by day's end!"

Miss Feynman bit her trembling lower lip and looked helplessly at Freya and me.

"What are you waiting for?" Mr Lamont said. "Go!" He raised his arm as though ready to strike the librarian. She whimpered and began gathering her things.

"As for the two of you," Mr Lamont snarled at Freya and me, "do not even consider leaving. I am not finished with you!" His dead eyes inspected me from head to toe. "And what has become of your uniform, young man?"

I raised a shaking finger and pointed at my ruined blazer, sitting on top of a pile of burnt books. Barely anything was left of the dusty, stew-stained, half-burned garment; just a few shreds of fabric held together by a couple of threads and maybe some cobwebs.

Mr Lamont picked it up and shoved it against my chest. "Total disrespect!" he said. "You will be disciplined twice as severely!" He looked around. "And what has become of that friend of yours?" he said.

Just beyond Mr Lamont, I caught a glimpse of Daniel, stepping out from behind the shelving.

"Gone to his next lesson, sir," I said quickly. "Said he no longer wished to squander school time and resources."

Mr Lamont let out a low growl.

Daniel mouthed "Thank you" at me and nodded. He slipped back behind the bookshelf, twirling the library key around his fingers, then vanished from sight.

Hold on ... Daniel ... "D"? Could he have been the one who ...?

But just then Mr Lamont grabbed Freya and me by the ears and began tugging us out of the door.

"Ow!" Freya yelped. She tilted her head sideways and squirmed. We stumbled into the hallway. It was almost pitch black. There were no other students around. Not a sound came from any of the classrooms. It was like we were the only ones left in school, stuck here with this madman.

"I hope you two are prepared!" Mr Lamont sneered.

Freya gulped. "Prepared for what?"

Mr Lamont looked Freya up and down as if she were mad. "Why, for your appointment with Thrasher, of course!"

CHAPTER 13

Mr Lamont dragged us ear-first through the archway towards his office. I hoped caning didn't hurt too much. I tried to console myself with the fact it couldn't be any worse than the time I took a ramp too hard at the skate park and landed flat on my face. Well, probably not.

I looked sideways at Freya. She was trembling. "It's OK, Frey," I said. "We'll get through this."

"I thought this whole thing would be done with

once we stopped the fire," she whispered. "I thought we'd be home by now."

So had I.

"No idle chatter!" Mr Lamont thundered as he tossed us into his office. I staggered to a halt on the red, green and gold carpet, rubbed my ear and glanced around. The room was almost identical to the one Mr Malton occupied – only without the computer and photographs. Instead, paintings of barren landscapes hung alongside portraits of gaunt bald men with sunken cheeks and lifeless expressions. Their eyes seemed to follow our every move.

Mr Lamont directed me to the corner of the room where a long, gnarled switch of wood rested against the wall. It had a thick handle and something that looked like tape holding it together in the middle. I wondered with a tremble how many times he'd broken it on some poor kid's backside. Thunder cracked outside and lightning flashed across the room. For a brief moment, Mr Lamont's black eyes seemed to glow bright red. My knees wobbled.

Mr Lamont's mouth pressed into a thin line and he pointed at Freya.

"You! Wait there while this one receives his beating," he said. "And you" – he shoved my back – "reach for your toes and accept your punishment!"

I sucked in a deep breath and glanced at Freya. She gave me a sad half-smile and mouthed "Good luck".

I nodded and bent down, waiting for the smack of the cane.

Instead, Mr Lamont's loud voice broke the silence. I glanced sideways, still clutching my ankles. "You!" he yelled at my sister. "OFF! MY! CHAIR!"

164

But it was too late. Freya was already lowering herself into the throne-like seat against the wall.

Mr Lamont's face turned red. He raised the cane high in the air. I started to feel woozy, as if the room was spinning; it was the same feeling I had had in here earlier. I heard the swish of the cane and squeezed my eyes shut tight, bracing for the blow.

Three, two, one . . . I counted to myself and waited.

. . . and waited . . .

Nothing happened.

I opened my eyes. My vision was blurred. I couldn't tell up from down, left from right.

It took a moment to register that Mr Lamont was gone. But Freya was still there, seated regally in the throne.

I stood up straight, blinked and looked around. The room had changed. There was the computer!

And pictures of Mr Malton and his family arranged on his desk!

Freya grinned at me. "It worked! I got us back!" she said. "You can thank me later."

Sunlight filtered through the window shades. I could hear birds chirping and cars rumbling down the street. It was morning. And we were alive!

"I can't believe it, Frey!" I said. "We spent the whole night in a haunted school ... and survived!" With a rush of relief I realised her freckles were back, as was the blue of her eyes and the red tints in her hair. I looked down at my hand and flexed it. Pink and warm. *Phew*.

"Yeah, that's pretty awesome." Freya jumped up from the chair, then slapped her forehead. "Except we are going to be in so much trouble! Mum must be freaking out!"

"Yeah, right," I said. "Mum . . . Hold on . . . I've got an idea."

I hurried over to Mr Malton's desk, slid open the top drawer and grabbed my phone.

Hi Mum, I texted. *Came to school early to hand in project. Freya with me, too. Hope u had fun last night.*

I waited for what felt like a thousand years, praying she hadn't gone into our rooms this morning and seen our us-shaped pillow-decoys under our duvets. Finally, the phone buzzed back. I glanced down.

OK dear, Mum wrote. *Pls make sure she eats breakfast. And remember, no peanuts!*

Good old Mum.

"We're fine," I said. I shoved the phone in my pocket and put my project down on Mr Malton's desk. I taped the photographs into my project at the speed of light, barely glancing at them. "We better get out of here before Malt-head arrives," I said, quickly shutting the folder.

A bell tolled eight times.

Freya raised an eyebrow.

"Is that what I think it is?" she said.

We walked to the window and peered outside. Where once there had sat a circle of bricks as monument to the old bell tower, the *actual* bell tower now rose high into the cloudless morning sky. "Weird . . . " I said. I spun back around and took a closer look at the black and white photographs on the wall. There was the photo from 1863. Except, no, wait . . . Now the label read "Class of 1864". Even stranger, they were all smiling. And there was Daniel, a big grin on his face, standing right next to . . .

"Miss Feynman?" Freya said.

The librarian stood at the centre of the picture,

clutching a book and smiling. Beneath it, I read: "Clara Feynman, headmistress."

"What happened to Mr Lamont?" Freya asked.

"Don't know," I said. "Really don't care." I scooped my project off Mr Malton's desk, glancing at my watch. "It's eight o'clock. Come on, let's get out of here."

We slipped out of the office and crept down the hall, crossing quickly into the new part of the building. Only, it didn't look so new any more. The place looked just as it had done in Victorian times: the floors were wood, the walls panelled.

My heart sank. "What's going on?" I said. "Are we still stuck in 1863?"

It made no sense. I opened a classroom door and peeked inside. Weird. There were the computers and white boards – not an ink well, blackboard or old desk in sight. Freya and I looked at each other in disbelief. Then, her eyes opened wide.

"Wait ... " she said. "Brendan, we did it!"

"Did what?" I asked.

"We saved the school!" she said. "It didn't burn down! Don't you see? That's why we were here last night. To save the school. And all those poor kids who died."

Could it be? Was Freya right? I glanced down the hall at the lockers lined up in their usual spots, then back at the old archway.

Two un-singed angels carved in wood smiled serenely back at me.

I smiled back. Somehow, we'd managed to save all the children from 1863. We were heroes ... the only pity was, no one would ever know it.

CHAPTER 14

Freya and I walked out of the front doors into the courtyard. The mist had lifted. The sun was shining bright. Never in my life had I been so happy to see daylight. Freya was chattering on about how weird the night had been and how no one would ever believe her, not in a million years. Personally, I didn't especially feel like telling anyone. The whole thing was just too creepy.

I turned and looked back at our school. The old Victorian building stood tall above the manicured

grounds, spires poking up into the clear blue sky. A pair of windows framed the doorway like a set of eyes, watching. I shivered, wondering who had stolen the project from my bag and sent me back to the school and back in time. Something flickered in a window. A pale face, perhaps. And then, just as quickly, it disappeared.

I guessed I'd never know.

"So, seriously," Freya was saying, "all that made me hungry." She patted her stomach. "I could really go for some bacon and eggs!"

I laughed.

"Yeah, me too," I said. "We have half an hour. Let's hit the café before school starts."

The tall iron gates to the school were now wide open, so we jogged straight through ... and collided head-on with Mr Malton.

The headmaster's briefcase flew from his hands, scattering papers across the ground. "For goodness' sake!" he huffed. He leaned over and picked up his things. The top of his hair flopped sideways and dangled there. I had to bite my lip to keep from chuckling.

"What are you two doing here so early?" Mr Malton stood and slapped his comb-over back into place. He looked us up and down. "And what in the devil are you wearing?"

"Oh, this?" I tapped the filthy blazer hanging from my shoulders. "I'm, uh . . . dressing in period costume. That's it! For my project!" I pulled the folder from my inside pocket. "And Freya and I came here early to hand it in to you. Personally. First thing in the morning. Just like you asked, sir."

Mr Malton raised an eyebrow and took the project

from my hands. "We'll just see ..." he said. He flipped the folder open. "Hmm ... well, how do you like that?" he said with a nod. "Very good! I'll admit, I didn't think you had it in you!"

A smug smile crept across my face. I couldn't help it: I knew once Mr Malton looked at my project I would get the grade I needed to avoid detention. I watched with satisfaction as Mr Malton flicked through the pages. But then his smile turned to a frown.

"Is this supposed to be some sort of joke?" His eyes narrowed.

"Joke?" I said. "I don't understand ..."

Mr Malton cut me off. "All this nonsense about a fire." He flipped more pages. "And students and teachers dying. Are you deranged?"

"Hey, now! That's not fair!" I said.

"And how did you fake these photographs?" Mr Malton asked. "Very clever," he said grudgingly, "to mock-up photos of the old school that no one's ever seen before." Then he harrumphed and said, "Here's one that I'm not surprised you included." I looked over his shoulder and to my shock there was a picture of Daniel, tongue out, eyes crossed, clutching Cook's cauldron. Freya gasped, and our eyes met. Was he sending us a message? A "hello" from the past?

Then Mr Malton scowled. "But this project was supposed to be *fact*, not *fiction*." He slammed the folder shut.

"But ... " I started to say. Then it hit me.

We'd stopped the fire. We'd saved the school.

And in the process, wrecked my homework.

My shoulders drooped. This was the most unfair thing that had ever happened to me! The one piece of homework I'd actually done, and done well, was ruined because I had stupidly gone back in time and saved the lives of, like, a hundred people.

Remind me never to do *that* again!

"You obviously have too much time on your hands," Mr Malton said with a nasty smile. "Perhaps you'd like to spend it with me in detention ... "

I braced myself. Maybe lifetime in detention wasn't the worst thing ever. It did beat Cook's stew. Or being locked in a bell tower. Or Mr Lamont's cane ...

"... for the next month," Mr Malton said. He shoved the folder against my chest. "While you write a *new* report."

"A new report?" I said. "That's so—"

"*Unfair?* Perhaps you'd rather spend *two* months in detention, then?" Mr Malton said.

"No, thank you," I said.

Mr Malton shook his head. Shuffling off up the pathway toward the main school building, we heard him mutter, "Kids these days . . . " Something about his limp looked strangely familiar. I shivered.

Freya snapped me out of that thought. "Well, that could've been worse," she said. "Maybe this time you want to take me up on the offer to write your project for you? You did promise me an escort to the Side Street concert, after all."

Trust her to fake her own death just to get me to that concert.

But, on the other hand, I had a pretty good idea of what I'd do for the new report. It just needed a little research . . .

Extract from

The First Headmaster of

Weirville School

by Brendan Jakes

Mr Edward Lamont was the first headmaster of Weirville School. He was known for his motto: "A healthy body equals a healthy mind", and for his devotion to science. It was, in fact, his devotion to science that led to his untimely and horrible death.

It was the night of 16 October, 1863, during a massive thunderstorm, that Mr Lamont decided to recreate Benjamin Franklin's famous experiment with electricity. Tying a key to the end of a kite, Mr Lamont stood in the school's courtyard and attempted to harness the awesome power of lightning. Sadly, the experiment went awry. Mr Lamont was electrocuted to death.

Upon Mr Lamont's passing, the school librarian, Miss Feynman, took over as headmistress. Well-regarded as a creative thinker ahead of her time, Miss Feynman turned the school into a centre of excellence for creative arts, especially writing.

In fact, one of Miss Feynman's star pupils – Daniel Mason – went on to become a prolific and well-respected author. His first novel, *The School Fire: A Ghost Story*, sold more than a million copies – and is still popular, even today.

However, the most coveted book is a first edition. Dedicated to "F", his "favourite feisty little redhead", it is autographed by Mr Mason himself with his trademark signature: a single letter, D.

A+ Excellent report! Lamont was a true credit to the profession. We should have more teachers like him in this day and age!